BLOOD TRAIL TO
TALL PINE

 This Large Print Book carries the
Seal of Approval of N.A.V.H.

A ROAMER WESTERN

Blood Trail to Tall Pine

Matthew P. Mayo

WHEELER PUBLISHING

A part of Gale, Cengage Learning

GALE
CENGAGE Learning·

Farmington Hills, Mich • San Francisco • New York • Waterville, Maine
Meriden, Conn • Mason, Ohio • Chicago

GALE
CENGAGE Learning·

LIBRARY OF CONGRESS CATALOGING-IN-PUBLICATION DATA

Mayo, Matthew P., author.
    Blood Trail to Tall Pine : a Roamer Western / by Matthew P. Mayo.
        pages cm. — (A Roamer Western; 1) (Wheeler Publishing Large Print
    Western)
    ISBN 978-1-4104-7183-3 (softcover) — ISBN 1-4104-7183-7 (softcover)
    1. Western stories. 2. Large type books. I. Title.
PS3613.A963B58 2014
813'.6—dc23   2014019357

Published in 2014 by arrangement with Cherry Weiner Literary Agency

Printed in the United States of America
   1 2 3 4 5   18 17 16 15 14

*For my parents, Gayla and Bill Mayo,
straight and true.*

Many and sharp the num'rous ills
Inwoven with our frame!
More pointed still we make ourselves
Regret, remorse, and shame!
And man, whose heav'n-erected face
The smiles of love adorn,
Man's inhumanity to man
Makes countless thousands mourn!
— "Man was made to mourn: A Dirge"
Robert Burns

CHAPTER ONE

My eyes snapped open in the strange gray light of early morning as a grizzly grunted hot breath in my face. It stank of death and rancid meat. I heard Tiny Boy, my Percheron stallion, neighing and thrashing in the undergrowth, hobbled and unable to run from this certain death.

I lay on my side, my Bowie knife just under my fingertips, the handle laced down with a rawhide strip. That's me to a T— safe at all costs. Only this time my caution could cost me my life.

The bear's face was inches from mine. It was still too dark to see well, but from where I lay on the ground looking up I saw the outline of its massive shaggy head and beyond that the wagging shoulder hump that quivered with every move the bear made, silhouetted against the lavender-gray sky.

I hoped it was still too dark for it to see

my fingertips work the simple knot and free the twelve-inch blade that might buy me a few seconds to roll away — if I landed well the first and only strike I was liable to get. To continue inhaling the rotted, stagnant breath of that primal beast as it snuffled and nosed me was one of the mightiest struggles I ever faced. I vowed if I made it out of this mess that I would give up sleeping out of doors. Or at least never again tie down my knife's handle. I'll promise anything in a situation like that.

The best I could hope for, I knew, was to sink a swift upward stroke at the very spot where the throat and chest meet. The growing light shone dull on the claws, curved surgical instruments a full four inches in length, as they scratched ever closer to my face. The eyes were hooded, buried deep in the big head, but its nose, a twitching creature all its own, worked at me like the trunk of an elephant. The bear grunted and a rumbling from deep within its body, like boulders crashing down a slope, grew louder the closer the bear drew to my face. If it got much closer, my head would be in its mouth. I kept my eyes slitted, looking through the lashes, and didn't breathe. It was then I noticed something odd about the grizzly's face, almost as though it shone.

I cursed myself for having rolled from my pistols in my sleep, which I always tucked under my blanket at my waist. They were now behind me, though how far I did not know. Nor did it matter, for any movement would trigger this beast's bullet-fast reflexes into play and I needed all the time I could buy, even if it meant mere seconds.

The knife was free and I curled my fingers around the horn handle. I played the intended motion in my mind and knew, though it was my only chance, that it was not going to work. I would succumb right here in my damn bed, wrapped in a blanket. And then the thing would maul me and drag me off half-dead and leaking everything that I was made of, to bury me in leaves and dirt and play with me for days before I fully expired. I vowed that though it was my fate I would not surrender to it without a fight at the outset.

In one motion I pulled on the knife and yelled for all I was worth, an amount at that moment that meant considerably more to me than any sack of gold, panniers filled with provisions, or deed to a fine big ranch.

The roar that burst from the beast stifled my own. Its thickly haired foreleg, already in motion, blocked my swing. I had thrust so hard that my forearm struck the bear's leg and the knife flew from my grasp, damaging nothing but my hopes for survival. The big foreleg arched at me, those claws slicing like knives, catching my buckskin shirt on the right shoulder as I rolled away from it and what I hoped was toward my pistols. As I rolled, kicking free my legs from my blanket and scrabbling at the dirt with my toes — my boots sat flopped by the now-dead cookfire — I grabbed where I remembered laying my gunbelt. But there was no time.

It was on me, bawling, a mouth wide and impossibly open — two heads could fit between those top and bottom jaws with their sets of ragged fangs. Its breath drove at me like heat blasting from a smithy's forge. I crabbed backward and it advanced on me, stalking, planting massive feet on either side of my arms as I skittered in retreat. It swung its head side to side in wide arcs, its voice ranging from growl to heavy breath. For a moment it was a standoff, as if the beast didn't quite know what to do with me.

I swung my right arm back, grabbing at anything and finding nothing, amazing to me considering I was in a small clearing full of shed pine branches. The beast roared again and leaned down at me, sniffing and grunting, and in the rising light for the first time I saw its eyes and they glowed. I must be dreaming, I thought. And then I saw the muzzle, the snout, and the shine I saw earlier was a face of mostly silver-white hair. And I knew that I was not dreaming, but was being attacked by an ancient and blind grizzly bear.

My immediate thought was an even more urgent conviction that flight might save me. But in the next instant the idea was quashed as in the growing light I realized that the bear, while old and blind, was in excellent flesh and seemingly in the full of his vigor. And a blind bear doesn't maintain such an upper hand in the savage natural world without relying heavily on other senses. This bear's nose, I reasoned, must be to blame for its perfect physique, despite its age and obvious infirmity. I would be no match for that nose, and coupled with a grizzly's speed, my time afoot would be brief.

Though the thought occurred to me, I had no time to wonder why the thing had not yet savaged me with that gaping maw. I vowed to capitalize on the edge it gave me. The bear itself was odd, blind and ancient, a true silverback. It lashed out with that clawed arm, caught me in the chest, the backs of its claws sliding up my face from

13

chin to eye. I was spun to the side and landed on my back, something jamming me painfully. I scrambled to roll over — my belly to the heavens was the last position I wanted to be in with a giant grizzly looming over me. And that's when my shaking hands landed on my gun belt, the very thing that poked me in the back.

By then the bear again lorded over me, its nose darting back and forth as if someone were working a string attached to the tip. I rolled but was trapped against a fallen tree. The bear reared back, those lumbering feet inching off the ground then driving down at me, the wide-open mouth descending like a guillotine blade. I had no time to squirm fore or aft and struggled to pull the pistols, one in each hand, free from the holsters, but there was no time. I raised them as the beast's rank breath once again closed on my face.

I cocked them and squeezed the triggers in one frenzied motion. I hardly heard the roar of the guns over the pounding of my own blood in my head and the grizzly's ungodly roar in my ears. The first two bullets seemed to have little effect on the beast. It came down on me with its bulk, its mouth snapping beside my head. I screamed, then gasped for air as the beast's full weight sagged down on me. Movement to either side was not possible. I was trapped. To one side of my head was the bear's, those massive jaws snapping and barking. To the other the stub of a branch as thick as a wrist. I could not move my head. So this was the end!

I still had the ability to work the hammers and triggers and I did so, emptying the revolvers into the beast. The bullets prevented the bear from tearing off my head, though it still moved atop me, slower now and the sounds from its jaws, now gnashing and reflexively snapping, were more reminiscent of angry, exhausted sighs than the hellish roars of seconds before.

I felt a wetness and knew it was the bear's lifeblood draining down on me. And still it thrashed even as it leaked its last. My face was muffled in a blanket of long, coarse hair. My mouth and nose were choked with it. The weight of the bear's body was too much for me. I could not draw in breath and what I had had been pushed from me when the bear dropped. I worked to move myself to the side, the bear's head still swinging wildly, its body thrashing, though it apparently had lost the use of its limbs. I pushed upward, my hands still gripping the guns, and tried to buy myself space to breathe. The beast slumped down enough so that my face was now exposed to the chill morning air. I opened my mouth like a beached trout, but could take in none of the life-giving element.

Whether from the pain of the pistols jerking into its wounds or the urges that drive a last effort at life, the great bruin arched its neck and bellowed all of its savage, pure nature into that one primeval sound that will echo in my mind until I, too, am made aware of my last moment of mortality.

I did not have the luxury of time to consider this, for in the next instant the bear's massive head pitched forward and its jaws, scissored open, slid down over my head. I felt the massive teeth poking the soft flesh of my face, the prodigious back teeth digging into my scalp, and then the visceral stink of a last, exhaustive breath wheezed from its mouth and washed down over my face, the stink of a thousand deaths invading my every sense. The grizzly was well and truly dead.

And so I, too, would die in this pose and it would not take long. I am no small man and am well muscled for my six-foot, four-inch frame, but I had no hope of shifting 1,200 pounds of dead grizzly bear, though my motivation was of the most urgent a man is liable to ever find: I wanted to live. I knew I had but seconds before losing consciousness forever.

The beast's blood slicked my hands and its fur enough that I was able, with considerable effort, to pull my right hand from its death grip on the pistol. The blood acted as grease on the lifeless fur and I expelled the last breath in my body in a grunt as my hand slid free from between our bodies. I felt the cold air on my hand as I scratched at the earth. My groping fingers were rewarded with nothing but pine needles and dirt. I reached up toward my head, intending to push at the bear's torso enough to afford my chest some respite from the deadly weight, but my hand clunked against the pistol-length nub of branch that had moments earlier prevented me from moving out of the beast's way as it fell.

I grasped it now with my already fleeting strength, the edges of my vision darkening. I pulled, twisting my head slightly as I did so, the dead bear's teeth digging deeper into my flesh. I heard a popping sound and because my body was so numb from the oppressive weight of the bear I couldn't be sure if it came from my surely broken chest or from the bear, or some combination of the two of us. And at that moment I did not care.

All I wanted was what began to leak into my gasping mouth — air. More pulling, fortified by my scant but increasing success and I was rewarded with a rush of crisp mountain morning air as the bear slid enough to my left to afford my lungs to resume their intended duties.

As the bear slumped sideways its head dragged with it, its jaws closing and pulling at the same time. My head was still between those yellow and black jagged stumps of teeth, and the largest of them, though the points were dulled by age and use, were still sufficiently pointed enough to peel my ears from my head. I pushed on the moist snout with the heel of my hand. It worked and I managed to raise the upper jaw and save my ear, though the pressure forced the lower teeth to dig deeper into my face. Fresh blood ran down my cheek and chin and into my mouth. It was my blood.

I gagged and tensed my facial muscles as much as possible, knowing the worst was yet to come. I had to get the great head pushed off mine and away. The pain increased but I managed to pry the gaping maw from me. The sudden weight of the bear's freed head flopping backward helped pull the entire body further off mine.

I lay there gasping, my chest rising and falling, my head swimming with great gouts of air that restored elixir of life. The bottom half of my body was still pinned by the bear but my arms were free. I could not move and my vision blurred then cleared, blurred again, and I heard a snapping sound to my right.

I looked that way and, as the darkening and blurring increased, I thought I saw a man, then another behind him. They were crouched and staring, not but a few strides away, and seemed to be floating, quivering there above the ground, the early light hinting at their features. Were they Indians? Bannock? Shoshoni? Blackfoot? Or just ghosts? Perhaps the great bear's spirit. . . . At that moment, though, I truly didn't care, for my sight went black and I lost all connection with the waking world.

That's how my day began. And then it got worse.

CHAPTER TWO

How long I lay like that I'm not sure. Images of who I was, who I am, floated in and out of my head like characters on a stage. I heard voices of men, women, children, old and young, all chanting the names hurled my way through the years. From the Yukon to Mexico, from Virginia to California I've been called drifter, vagabond, wanderer, rover, rambler, restless spirit, no-good tramp, and others I won't repeat. A few of them are appropriate, I'm sure. The harsher-spirited folks usually preface the name with the word 'ugly.' The name given me by the woman who birthed me is 'Scorfano,' Italian for 'homely one.' And with a face like mine, I reckon I've earned it.

I thought of Maple Jack, the trapper with whom I spent much time. Years before, when I was sixteen, he'd saved me from freezing to death in a blizzard in the Rockies, and he became one of the few folks I ever formed a strong bond with. Though I did tell him my given name, I made it plain that I preferred to be called something else. He took to calling me 'Roamer' in much the same way an uncle might call a nephew 'youngster' or 'boy'. I don't mind the name — it suits me.

When a man's natural inclination is to be left alone, coupled with the fact that a face like mine is more closely associated with outlaws and bad men thinking bad thoughts and doing dark deeds, the suspicions of good folks are naturally aroused. From what I can tell it's a basic animal tendency to be with others of one's kind, to be part of a community. But I prefer my own company.

And that's another reason why I'm regarded with suspicion. I don't hate being around other folks, but I'm always relieved when it's time to part. Perhaps one day that will change. Considering the way I look and the way I feel, I'll be regarded with suspicion for some time to come yet. And I guess I don't mind. It keeps me moving, keeps me searching, though for what I'm not exactly sure.

I have no idea how long I was unconscious, but I awoke surprised. I expected to not awaken at all. I thought the drifting I was doing, the images of places and people

I had seen bouncing through my mind were the tag ends of my life before it fizzled away.

But I awakened to find that the vision I had when I was losing consciousness was partially true. I had seen what I took to be men hovering nearby. They weren't an illusion or the spirit of the beast I had slain (that had nearly exacted an equal revenge on me). They were real flesh-and-blood men. From their ruddy skins, darkened like the worn walnut of a gunstock, they might be Indian or even Mexican, though I doubted they would be so far north. No, they were probably half-breeds, though so crusted with dirt, grease, and grime I'm not sure how they stood each other's company.

I came around to find the smaller, younger-looking of the two watching over me. The other, older and thicker and wearing a huge, trail-weary hat with a tall crown, was skinning the bear. They had dragged it off my legs and he had the job halfway finished a few feet from me. I could have jumped him if I had the strength. He glanced up from his messy task, showing no concern. He might as well have been playing poker. I was no threat.

"Mister, you are one lucky fella. From the looks of you, though, you've been in more than one tangle with a killer grizz. Looks to me like you been worked with a ugly stick a few times, too!" Grimy the younger laughed so long and loud at his observations that even the somber skinner looked up at him. I barely heard it. Same old story. I was born ugly and now I'd die even uglier, thanks to the bear. My head throbbed. I didn't dare touch my cheek where I knew I would find long gashes and punctures from claws and teeth.

Though it was an old grizzly, its fur rippled and shone as the skinner struggled in peeling it back. It would make a warm and handsome coat and an even more valuable skin to sell, considering its unusual coloring. Most grizzlies didn't make it that far in age in such good health. Maybe this one had turned gray sooner than his time. I grunted as I reached out to prop myself up against the log.

Full morning light cracked through the treetops and a lone patch of gold worked its warming magic on my chest and arm. I looked down at it and saw the blood from the grizzly, forming a skin the color of slow-cooked kidney beans, thick on my torso and legs. It was so thick, in fact, that I couldn't make out my buckskins underneath. I closed my eyes and tried to speak but it came out as a sort of croaking sound. I licked my lips and tried again. "I can skin my own bear. But I thank you for your concern."

The older one looked at me again and resumed his task. He worked around the back feet, a tricky spot. I couldn't have been unconscious all that long. The carcass and blood steamed in the chill air of the early spring morning. I shivered. Without its thick coat a skinned bear looks an awful lot like a naked man. It never fails to startle me.

The grimy young one laughed and said, "Ain't your bear now, fella. It's ourn." He smiled and showed off the green and black stumps of what remained of his teeth. His jaw worked a quid and he spat a plume of thick brown juice at me. I flinched and every muscle in my body stiffened as if I were made of wood. The juice hit the ground by my hand and spattered, like rain off a rock, against me.

I stared at the man, my predicament slowly dawning on me. I am usually a touch sharper in the mornings, though only if I have had my coffee before I kill my morning bear. Grimy giggled at me, filthy hands hooked in his belt, two revolvers, what make I wasn't yet sure, were tucked in there, backward fashion, which always struck me as impractical and not a little awkward.

24

He wore an odd assortment of clothing, as if pieced together from a variety of wardrobes, and atop his head sat a bowler style hat. I've never been partial to such a topper. Silly as it sounds, it changes my entire opinion of a man, from one of promise to one of weakness.

He regarded me, his rangy bottom jaw working his chaw in a slow, cowlike manner. I knew he was going to speak before he did. And I knew about what he was going to say.

"You are about the ugliest fella I ever did see. Forget what the bear done to you, mister you got a head like a bastard kitten and twice as nasty, no lie." He shook his head and spat again.

I knew why he stared, of course. In fact, I was used to it. You grow accustomed to most anything if you've lived your entire life with it. And my homely face has been with me since birth, when I was handed to my mother. She looked at me and screamed, "Diavolo!" — the Italian word for 'devil.' Then she gave me to the cook to raise, no matter that I was the first-born. I grew up thinking I was merely the stable boy on my parents' Virginia estate.

If there is a specific look to outlaws and ne'er-do-wells, then I must have it. I'm on the large side, north of six feet tall. I'm well muscled and I have a big block head topped with short curly black hair. My head is wide, my eyes maybe too narrowly set, my nose bent to one side and my upper lip is not as most people's. It never quite formed fully on its own. A cleft palate, they call it. It doesn't affect my speech or my eating or drinking, but it affects my looks and so it affects my relationships with my fellow men and women. So much so at times that I keep to myself as much as possible.

I also have a few scars on my face that I earned in close skirmish in the war, though no one wants to hear that. But I'd have to agree with people if they were basing the outlaw look on my eyes alone. They're dark, no getting around it. I've been told they're merciless, but I prefer thoughtful.

"Why?" I asked, nodding at the bear, but really at the situation in general, and hoping to distract Grimy from staring open-mouthed at me. It worked.

Grimy giggled again as if I'd told him he was wealthy beyond his dreams and that he'd live forever. "Why, you ask?" he said. "Why would a dead man need anything other than a patch of dirt to stretch out on?"

"Then you plan on killing me?"

"That's the plan, yessir." He pushed my

flopped boots with his own, regarding them as one would a potential purchase. "Maybe even take your head with me. Bound to be a bounty on one such as yourself. I think I seen the posters."

The other man, similar enough to Grimy in looks it occurred to me they might be brothers, looked up at him from peeling the last of the hide back, and shook his head no, then resumed skinning the old bear.

I was too exhausted and sore to allow the full impact of my predicament to settle on me yet. All I could do was stare him down, and after a fashion I said, "At least leave me my horse." I hadn't seen Tiny Boy, but doubted he'd gotten far with hobbles on. I hoped he hadn't hurt himself.

I told you I wasn't the most impressive fellow until I've had my coffee. They ignored me. By then I'd revised my opinion of the two thieves and decided they were not Indian in blood, but just needed a good scrubbing.

The taller of the two rolled the fresh bear skin and secured it behind the cantle on the saddle of one of their horses. I also noticed that my missing gunbelt and pistols were buckled and slung over the horn of the same saddle. Dried blood clung to the guns and belt. The other thief was slicing hunks of meat from the bear. Thoughts of the delicious wonder that is a properly cooked piece of bear left me feeling hungry.

Grimy looked down at him as one might on a child who just embarrassed a father. "Oh, all right," he said, folding his arms over his chest and scowling at me. "My brother's almighty impressed with you and how you handled the bear. He says that anybody can deal with a bear in such a way deserves a shot at livin'. I ain't so easy to impress but I'll give this one to him."

How he knew what his brother said when I hadn't heard a word pass between them was a mystery. While Grimy the Younger pouted with his back to me, and with his brother busy, I inched myself backward to more of a sitting position. I looked for my knife to the right, past the spot where I'd slept and where the fight had begun. If they hadn't seen the blade, it was over there somewhere in the pine needles a good ten feet from where I lay. In my physical state, sopping with stiffening bear blood and with a chest that offered me a pair of sharp pains, one on each side of my rib cage, I guessed I wouldn't be making any sudden moves for the knife. Especially not when I was surrounded by two armed thieves.

I contented myself with working my arms

up and down, stretching out the kinks as best I could, and exploring the four gashes in my shoulder where the bear's claws had ripped through my buckskin shirt as if it were newsprint. The more I moved, the more various parts of my body throbbed. My head ached like something that had almost been squashed in the jaws of a giant beast, and I tenderly probed with my fingertips the various scratches and punctures my head received from the teeth of the brute. That's what I needed, I thought. More scars and distinguishing marks.

To tell you the truth I was still in a bit of a daze most of the time the thieves plundered me dry. I knew what they were doing and why they were doing it, but I was so sore and shaken from my encounter with the bear, and I was so amazed that I lived through the experience, that I had a difficult time feeling too concerned about my future woes.

"Take the bear and leave me and my things be," I said. The two men looked at me. The older one hadn't opened his mouth up to that point but he heard me.

Grimy certainly did. He turned around from sulking in the trees and snorted. "One more crack from you and it won't matter if you whupped a hundred grizzlies, I'll do you one right twixt the eyes."

The man at the horse stepped up beside Grimy. He had a good four inches on the dirtier man and he stared down at him with ice in his eyes. Grimy broke the deadlock and walked away, muttering, "I guess we'll take what we want to take."

I was grateful for the hard-looking fellow, but I knew he was no friend. He finished cinching a canvas-wrapped bundle of bear meat tight with rope and turned immediately to my traps. The other joined in. My old saddle and saddle bags, blankets, coffee pot — they packed up the lot, loading most of it on Tiny Boy. How I missed seeing the big brute I'm not sure, but he must have been lined up there the entire time.

Something told me they weren't just being helpful to an invalid. They secured the lot with ropes and then Grimy the younger mounted up. They conferred amongst themselves. Grimy turned to me and scowled as if I had insulted him, then rode off with my big Percheron reduced to the role of pack animal loping behind. I watched him go with a stab of regret. Tiny Boy was more than a horse big enough to carry me. He was a true companion who never judged me by anything more than how I treated him. I wish people were more like that.

The older, quiet brother rebuilt my little fire ring that scattered when the bear and I rolled through it. He coaxed a few stray coals into flame with the help of his breath and gathered hairy tinder. His hands, calloused and used to hard work, moved with an adroitness that belied their gnarled appearance. He dragged the scattered remnants of my scant firewood pile close to the ring and pointed to the sprawled and hacked carcass of the bear and nodded. Those same ice-gray eyes regarded me for a moment, then he turned and walked to his own horse, mounted, and rode away in the direction of his brother. I watched the top of that tall hat as it wound through the trees and out of sight.

They left me my boots and didn't molest my person looking for hidden money, unless they did so before I'd revived. I waited until they were well away from there to check my coin purse for certain. It would be in the nature of that filthy fellow to keep a sharp eye and come back to finish me off. I had the spirit, if not the means, to survive. And if I survived, I vowed I would find the thieves and deal with them in my own way.

CHAPTER THREE

Except for the highest reaches on this spur of the Rockies, the snow was gone until fall and new leaves whispered together in a slight breeze far above. I was thankful it was late spring.

I was a mess, and though I didn't think any of my more vital bones were broken, my arms and legs might as well have been, considering my lack of mobility. For half an hour after the renegades stripped my camp clean and left me to die in that glade by the river, I was little more than bear bait. If I was this sore now, I thought, I dreaded waking up the next day, for that's when muscles let their owner know how displeased they've become about the travails they were put through the day before. Mine had been so taxed I wondered if they would stop working altogether.

After a spell of brooding about my lousy plight, I decided to do something about it.

I've never been one to lament for too long anyway. I figure it's time spent on something that makes me feel worse about whatever it is I'm already feeling low about. Seems to me the point of feeling bad is to get yourself to feel better as soon as you can.

While I set about standing up and shaking loose the knots in my legs and arms I took stock of my remaining possessions. There was the coin purse about my neck that the thieves didn't find. For whatever reason they had, at least they hadn't pilfered from my person. I retrieved the rawhide purse, lifting it out from under my sopping bloodied shirt, and untied the mouth. A dozen coins and two nuggets of gold each the size of a man's back tooth rolled into my palm. Nearly twenty dollars in cash, and the gold was worth another forty to fifty.

The nuggets were my safety money. I also had four more similar size nuggets sewed into my saddle, back under the cantle. It would take a man a month of Sundays and heap of a lot more curiosity and patience than I would ever have in order to find them. I shook my head and shrugged. Unless I found my saddle and hopefully Tiny Boy under it, then my safety funds amounted to what was in my coin purse. Could be worse. I stuffed the bloodied little sack back down inside my shirt and stretched my arms, wincing every time the broken ribs were discomfited.

I hadn't seen either of them using my knife. The blade used by the skinner paled in comparison to mine, which was both bigger and of a finer grade of steel, thus able to sustain an edge for a longer period of time. If they had found my knife they would have used it to help skin the bear. A twinge of hope fluttered in my chest. Of course it might also have been another sore muscle making itself known, but I'll take my glimmers where and how they show themselves.

I inched my way to the end of the log and groped there in the leaves and needles until I laid a hand on the blade of my long horn-handle knife, where it landed when my attempt at stabbing the beast came to naught. Never had I been so glad to heft a tool. It would certainly make my life easier and might even help to save it. I wiped the soil from the blade and slid it into the blood-soaked sheath on my waist. I'd clean the blood from it later. But right now I had to clean the blood from me. It was beginning to cake, flaking and setting into my shirt and the tops of my britches. I was thankful it wasn't hotter out. I thought of the desert and had to laugh, picturing a massive grizzly bounding across dunes after a sprier version of myself.

If not for my missing horse and goods I would have guessed that those thieves were the spirit of that great bear himself seeking a little compensation for what I took from him. I almost wanted to believe that. I was afoot in the wilderness, and while I am not prone to carrying all that much in the way of possessions, I knew I would miss certain ones of them, namely my scant but cherished collection of books. And Tiny Boy's company, of course. Though possessions and horse aside, I had a bad case of grudge and I wanted satisfaction.

If it wasn't for that very human urge for revenge, then I could as easily have considered myself lucky to be alive, and it being springtime, I could have headed on my somewhat chosen route northwest, eventually found a settlement and bought, bartered, trapped, and traded for a new outfit. And maybe even a book or two, if luck was with me.

I had the luxury of spring and summer before me, short though they are in the mountains. But it was not to be and I knew it. I would try to find those men. My too-human trait of anger and justice was still much with me and I blame all that happened to me over the next week on that poor decision. If only I had known, I would have walked northwest.

By the sun's steady creep upward I knew it was mid morning. My camp had been a good one for nearly a week and I hated to leave it. It was a relaxing place to not do a whole lot and that's exactly what I had been up to. I had game aplenty and all my gear was repaired and cleaned. That sticking hammer on my Henry finally got the greasing it needed. The two holes in my favorite blanket, the dark brown one — it was thicker than the other — were sewn tight, and I even shaved clean two days ago.

And in all of that I still had time to reread, for the thousandth time, bits of Homer's *The Odyssey,* Shakespeare's collected works, and the Holy Bible. I have read a fair amount of books since I was a boy, most of them before leaving the place I was raised, but many since, and I have found that these three bring me the greatest pleasure and continue to offer me new notions, sometimes days after I've spent time with them.

Certainly the loss of my rifle, revolvers, and horse, as well as my cookware and spare clothes, was a major blow, but I believe it was the books that I felt hardest. I'd had them a long time. Aside from the knife, my copy of *The Odyssey* was the only possession I still had from when I left home all those years ago. I rested my bloodied hand atop the big knife's steel hilt and took a deep breath, trying to fill my lungs beyond the sharp pains of what I guessed were broken ribs. I've had such breaks a couple of times in the past and the only thing for them is to take it easy and let them knit on their own.

I tossed sticks on the waning campfire and grabbed my fallen boots — no way was I going to chance losing any of my scant but vital possessions now. I stiff-legged my way barefoot down the little trail I had made to the river's edge. The river was actually a tributary off the mighty Callahoon, though it was big enough to navigate a canoe in. I dropped the boots and lowered myself down to my knees in the mud. It took some doing but I managed to peel off that stinking, godawful, blood-stiffened buckskin shirt.

I shucked the pants before I slid into the water — wet buckskin is not all that easy to take off. As I worked them down my legs my hands felt the little bulge in a front pocket. My heart gave an extra beat when I realized what it was. My flint and steel. I could make fire. I plucked out the hide-wrapped tools and slid them down inside a leaning boot, followed by my knife, and even my coin purse. I didn't plan on being any further from my treasure trove than a few feet as I bathed in the shallows.

The water was cold at the edge, and when I finally worked into it fully it was as shocking to the system as being awakened by the world's largest blind grizzly bear looking to eat me. Well, maybe not quite that shocking, but it was a hearty burst to the system.

As I scrubbed myself with a handful of sand — a mountain man named Shine once told me it stimulates and brings a fire to the skin, and he's not half wrong — I took stock of my worth. First and foremost I was alive. Next, I had money enough to set me up in basic gear, if in a modest fashion and if I wanted to mingle with mankind again. Though at present I saw that I had little choice. Third, I had my trusty knife. I also had boots and clothes. I could walk without shredding my feet on the rough terrain ahead. And I also had my flint and steel. I could walk, kill, make heat, and it was spring, so I wouldn't freeze to death. All in all, I thought, I was in better shape than when I came into the world.

When my body was as clean as I could

make it, I started in on my clothes, which I had soaking in the water with me. After a half-hour of scrubbing with sand it was obvious the blood left permanent stains. I didn't mind so much, considering the alternatives — grim indeed.

I spent all of that day at the campsite doing little other than cooking bear meat, preparing as much as I could for carrying, gathering firewood, and twice I walked to the river to drink. Before dark I dragged that old silverback's carcass as far from camp as I could, anticipating hungry predators in the night. The last thing I needed was another run-in with nature's violent side.

But despite my best efforts, shortly after full dark the beasts arrived. I had hacked pine boughs and gathered leaves both as a bed and as a covering for myself against the night's chill air.

I heard the snorting and snuffling, the faint rustling of leaves before I saw the glowing eyes and heard the panting. The wolves had come. It was the carcass they were after. I had dragged it away from the fire but not far enough, I realized. It was a heavy thing and I was a bedraggled thing and the two didn't get on so well. I kept the fire burning and sat up against the log, boughs and leaves piled around me, my knife at hand, and a number of arm-length branches with their ends in the fire and ready to grab should the need arise. I sat that way, feeding the fire and listening to the snarling and snapping of the wolf pack feeding on the remains of the beast that had almost killed me.

The slavering beasts resented my presence, I knew. They resented my fire and my smells, despite the cloying scent of bear blood that still clung to my clothes. They also smelled my own meat cache, which I decided to keep with me instead of raising into a tree, despite the danger of attracting predators. I was in no shape to climb trees and besides, I reasoned, that was no guarantee that some other beast wouldn't find my stash. I had no ropes from which to hang it.

With my knife I had gouged a hole in the ground beside the fire and wrapped the meat as best I could in layers of leaves and stripped bark, then buried it. Despite the savage sounds of the wolves my chin dropped to my chest a number of times out of exhaustion. Each time a yip would snap it back up and jerk my eyelids open as if they were operated on a pull string. If ever there was a night when I could have used a pot of strong, black coffee, it was that night.

And if ever there was a night when I had earned sleep, it was that night.

But I remained sleepless save for snatches of light slumber grabbed as shadows and shapes stood out against the gray of the earliest hours of dawn. By the morning's first light shafts I could see the picked-over bones of the grizzly and it looked less like a man and more like a museum's recreation of some creature of a distant time. Nothing but paw prints could be seen on the ground about the great bone rack. Even the deep contours of the head had been picked nearly smooth.

I worked my hands over my face, now more pock-marked and cut and scarred than it had been, thanks to grandpa grizzly. At least I could grow a beard I thought, then snorted. It had never done me any good. I was still regarded as frightening and strange no matter where I went.

I stretched my limbs and dreaded what terrors my body had in store for me this morning. Coffee would go a long way today in helping this sore body to ease into the day. Nothing for it but to do it, I thought, and pictured myself leaping to my feet. It didn't quite work that way and it was a full minute before I could unbend my knees and elbows and stand fully erect. With each effort I heard snaps and pops and felt the protests of hundreds of contracted muscles. I sounded like a sack full of sticks being stepped on. I felt like it, too.

After I visited the bushes and then the river, I roused the fire and warmed a decent chunk of meat, though I didn't eat too much for fear of running out of food before I could again procure a firearm of some sort. A gun might not be necessary hunting equipment for a lot of the Indians, but then again I hadn't met one who wouldn't opt for it over a bow, knife, or spear. I'd also seen a lot of half-starved Indians when the braves had bad luck on hunting parties. Once again I vowed revenge on the thieving duo.

After eating I rigged up a sort of basket of green branches, bark, and leaves to carry my store of meat, a handle topping it all off. A small feeling of satisfaction went a fair way toward warming me on the inside, though unbidden thoughts once again returned to coffee.

I shook my head and forced myself to instead think of my plans. They were simple. I would follow the river south until I reached the nearest settlement. It had been years since I'd made it down that way, my own ventures keeping me north for the past few seasons, and far west and south prior to that. But I seemed to recall a trading post of some sort south of where I was. Not the place I would normally head for, but then again it might serve my needs. And my needs were few. A rifle and a horse. Anything I could find beyond that would be a leg up in helping me to track my thieving friends.

As I watched the fire give up its ghost, I felt that same small pang of regret I get right in my bread basket whenever I take another creature's life. Fire always seems as much a living thing as a beaver or elk or raccoon or rabbit. Come to think of it, a river, too, has the same properties as fire. It's always moving, never looks quite the same, and it can kill you as quick as you let it. But they both can also keep you alive, as anyone who's ever been afoot in a hot place or stranded in a blizzard knows.

I urinated on the campfire and kicked dirt over the steaming coals, then packed more dirt on that. Another thing Maple Jack taught me. He is always particular about ensuring that a fire is good and out. As a young man he barely survived a fire that burned the wilderness for as far as the eye could see. Or so he told me. He was prone to pushing and pulling the edges of a story now and again, but he was also a mighty persuasive old man and his words about flame and a great many other things have stayed with me all these years.

Thoughts of old Maple Jack pulled me from my reverie. I gathered my little bundle of food and gave one last look-see at the campsite where I was almost killed by a dead bear. Then I trudged south along the riverbank.

CHAPTER FOUR

A day had passed since I left that bad-luck camp behind me. I made my way slowly through the pines along the edge of the river, years of fallen needles providing a spongy surface for walking. The air that morning was crisp and now that I was up and moving, warmth worked itself into my aching body and filled my stiff joints with a good fire. I spent the night within view of the river, its unending rush sounding like a crowd of great birds flapping together. I sat leaning against the broad trunk of a rough old white pine, my hips cradled between humped, bony roots like legs themselves.

I knew I would be sore and stiff the next morning and I figured if I started halfway upright it might make getting to my feet an easier task. It wasn't quite that simple, but sleeping in a sitting position helped. It still took me half an hour to work the stiffness out of every limb, finger, and toe. My neck, though, throbbed as I walked along, and it was no wonder. From the thudding cannon-fire in my head, I knew that it would be a few days before it didn't hurt to open my eyes fully. At least the thieves left my hat. Crushed and battered as it was its wide brim served to keep the patchy sun from my squinting eyes.

I chewed a strip of bear meat and as I walked, in no hurry — and good thing, as my sore limbs would not abide a faster pace — my thoughts once again circled back to a topic that I try to leave well enough alone, though I'm unsuccessful. Death. I've come close to my final moment on a number of occasions and for a few days following each time my thoughts will betray me and ride rough-shod over the intention I have set out for myself in this life, namely to keep to myself and get lost in the wide-open West.

It seems that, despite my own stated claims, there is a part of me buried deep who yearns for the very things I travel away from — family, friends, the closeness of a community, the predictability of a life lived in one place, the unparalleled companion-ship of siblings. I thought of the two broth-ers who had robbed me. As vile as they seemed, they meant something to each other. I, on the other hand, mean something only to myself. But when had it ever been otherwise? My entire life had been lived largely in solitude. Even as a child when I was among many people daily, I was a lone figure.

Lost that morning in these well-tramped trails of reverie deep inside my mind I failed to see the river's fork. I thought I would find it that day and I promised myself that I would pay attention enough that I might recognize it and bear left. I wanted to head East to reach the settlement I recalled hearing of some time before. I suspected it was the closest town to me. In fact I had half-planned to head there when the shine of the solitude of my camp wore off. I needed supplies, namely coffee, and I reasoned that a small town would have what I needed and little else. Perfect for me.

The day passed as if I was in a dream state. I have come close to that feeling twice before. Once when I was in the desert, convinced I was to die soon for want of water. The second time, I was invited to participate in a sweat-lodge ceremony with the Shoshoni, a small band of warrior natives who accepted me into their clan because I helped one of them after he was nearly killed by a buffalo.

But this feeling was not quite the same.

This time I was in the wilderness with plenty of water. The difference was that my body was in rough shape. I would have liked nothing better than to lay down. With every step I took away from what had once been one of the most pleasant camps I had set up in years, my body and mind willed each other to stretch out on those soft, bronze pine needles and sleep. But I knew that if I gave in to that sort of thinking I would make my task of survival even more difficult.

And I also held tight to the notion, no matter how slight it seemed, that if the little town I seemed to recall from years before was still there, it was the closest settlement to where I was and so the place the two thieves would likely make for. The chance of finding them was slim, to be sure, but it was there. And those were all the odds I needed.

Thanks to them I was relieved of the burden of carrying possessions. Small solace. I was alive, yes, but I could have used the little bundle of medicinal herbs I had in the saddlebags. Searches that morning turned up enough arnica for me to make a poultice. It helps with sore muscles when boiled and applied hot. But I had so many sore spots on me that I didn't know where to start. And I didn't have enough to dose myself all over, so I chewed on it, spitting it out when I felt I had ground the goodness from it.

With the sun offering its full strength, I stopped to drink from the river. I knelt slowly and eased myself down onto my chest with care, fully aware that one sudden twist and my broken ribs would send me into spasms of pain I didn't care to repeat. My mind was full of cotton batting, my eyes offering a wavering view of what lay ahead, as if they were filled with tears. All the result of fatigue and fear of the fact that if I didn't continue moving forward, I would have a particularly rough time of it. I doubted I would die out there in the wilderness, I had spent far too long alone in the woods for that to happen. I was far from any tribes I was familiar with, and the odds of running across an old chum like Maple Jack were as remote as me being attacked by a blind silverback grizz.

I chuckled at that, my voice out of place and raw sounding to me, as it always was when I had been alone for long periods. I slurped the water from my hands. And then I saw it, not two feet away in the water, a rainbow trout as thick as my forearm and as long as my entire arm, the current eddying above his topmost fin. I paused, water dripping from my lips and chin and hands. I gauged my chances of catching him. He was holding there in the current, his tail moving slowly side to side in that unhurried way only creatures of the wild have. Hawks soar this way, unbroken horses run this way, and fish swim this way. They know something I hope one day to learn.

The bank beneath me was an overhang where the current had cut in for years. The water there was dark and deep. But the silty brown bottom rose rapidly so that where that fat trout lay the water was no more than a foot deep. I could already hear the small campfire crackling, could smell the sweet tang of his flesh broiling on a stout stick, could already taste the flaking meat as it separated from the delicate rib bones and passed over my lips into my mouth. I licked my lips. I wanted that fish. Wanted him as bad as I ever wanted anything in my life. More than my first Henry rifle. More than that pudgy prostitute in Topeka. The one with the little white scar along her top lip and the long curling black hair that smelled of prairie flowers.

My aching torso stretched beyond the point of turning back, the weight of my upper body pulled me further over the water. For a moment I saw my hands, extended deep into the clear current before me, the cuffs of my buckskin still the same sandy color as the dry part of the sleeves above the water, my hands so pale and swollen they looked as if they belonged on the corpse of a man twice my size. And beyond them the fish held, the rich tones of his speckling altering with each slight twist of his body.

In the water, distance is deceiving. I knew this, but for the moment I had forgotten it, and I did not care. For in that sliver of time between a decision and a reaction, I was convinced of my success in catching that fish. And then my shadow darkened clear through to the gravel bottom.

And the truth, in a jester's hat, leered at me. I was too weak and too stiff and too tired to put up half the effort a man needs to catch such a magnificent creature bare-handed. I knew even at the best of times, with no injuries and my wits not dulled by fatigue, that fish could still sense my efforts and dart like a ricochet rifle shot into a deeper pool a few feet away, though it might as well be half the world away for all the good it would do me. But it was too late.

I slipped forward into the water with the quietest oath I ever uttered, knowing I had no one to blame but myself. Even before my arms speared all the way into the river, the fish whispered away. And I plunged straight onto the spot he had occupied.

The shock did me more good than harm. I moved faster than I thought possible and gained my feet within a few seconds after tumbling into the cold mountain water. Down in the flats it may have been nearing summer, but here, in hills fed by mountain streams, it was still cold enough to peel a man's breath from his lungs in a second.

I was back out of the water in less than a minute. As the day had turned off warm, and the trees were thinning the further south I traveled, I decided to not build a fire and instead walk until I was dry.

I reckoned that walking to warm up was better for my newly awakened limbs than sitting down by a campfire and risking my joints seizing and my teeth rattling together. I clumped on and on and my buckskins and boots dried stiff and I gradually slipped back into my fuzzy thinking, and that is when I must have lost track of which branch of the river I was traveling. When it did occur to me, I took solace in the fact that the river was still to my right, and so I was traveling in what I hoped was my intended direction.

■ ■ ■ ■

As I emerged from the thinning trees the sudden appearance of a valley below was akin to being offered a glimpse of paradise. Rolling plains of young grasses silvered in the wind and all about me foothills gave way to mountains, treed most of the way up their slopes. The branch of the river I followed had worried me. It narrowed at points to half its previous width. But it did angle eastward, and now that I was faced with the open promise of this lush place, I was convinced that I would find some sort of settlement in an easterly direction.

Far below, narrow twin trails curved along the river and then veered from it to venture west and out the other end of the little green valley. It was a road traveled by wagons. My eyes followed the trail to the east, beyond where it paralleled the river, and I lost it in the green mass below. My angle was too steep to see it well, but I guessed where it would be, and I could see the river's glint now and again from behind the grasses that hid it from me.

As I walked along, leaving the tree line behind, the wind increased, and in mere minutes the sky dimmed to the color of a bruise — not promising. The warm, sunny day with blue skies of a few hours before slipped behind a silent darkening shade that crept from the surrounding mountaintops inward over the little valley. From the west, a bank of thunderheads rolled east like massive ocean waves, raking the mountaintops with long tendrils of sheeting rain.

And then I saw, far and small in the distance, the defined angles of manmade structures. The town. It may well have been the settlement I remembered, situated as it was on a fine little river, but its most striking feature is the valley itself, though it did not ring any bells of familiarity with me. Not that it mattered in the least. With a renewed vigor I loped unsteadily down the slope to follow the river into town.

The closer I drew, hurried onward by the increasing wind at my back, the more I mused on the fact that as much as I have determined I need to spend my life in my own company and distinctly away from congregations of other people for long stretches of time, I was also looking forward to what this town could offer. I was sore, tired, and hungry. I resolved that if I couldn't find solutions to those ailments down there, then I would follow the trail West to the next town and find what I needed in it. But despite the stormy weather coming in fast, I conjured in myself a good, warm feeling about this little town, and I stepped up my pace.

I should have turned around.

CHAPTER FIVE

Over the foamy rim of my near-drained mug of beer, I kept my eyes fixed on the barkeep's jowly face. The big man stared back for a moment, then looked away, folding his drying rag. The same rag, I noted, that he had used to wipe the tobacco that pooled on the shelf of his chin. And it was the same rag he had wiped each glass with since I entered. No wonder the beer had an extra tang to it. I decided to nip that thought in the bud while I still had an appetite.

"Do you serve food here?"

The barkeep, his back to me now, wiped at his bottles with more vigor than he had in years, judging from the layer of greasy dust over everything back there. The only spots that gleamed in the place were on the bar where elbows rested. I ate another pickled egg while I waited for an answer. I was grateful that they had the jar of eggs, but they would have to work harder to fill me up. I hadn't exactly starved on my three-day walk here from the campsite, but brined eggs weren't what I had in mind as I trekked.

He looked me over again, his piggy eyes scrunching up and his mouth going tight as if he hadn't done the same thing five minutes before when I first walked in. I know what he was looking at and I probably would have done the same thing to him had I been in his overworked boots. Lightning filled the room with stark light as we stared at each other. Thunder followed it within seconds. The heart of the storm was nearly on us. Rain blew in sideways above and below the batwing doors. No one moved to close the inner doors.

My attire was not impressive, I knew. My buckskins were rank with sharp odors and stains despite my best efforts in the stream to clean them of grizzly gore. Even the subsequent dunking I took in pursuit of that elusive trout hadn't done much to smooth my appearance. And thanks to the rain, I was once again soaked to the bone. I had not made it to town before the rain began. Being wet didn't bother me half as much as the prospect of being the only thing standing in the bowl of all that green space as the inevitable lightning searched for an easy way to get to earth. With that in mind, I made it to the town just in time.

Thunder and lightning barreled from west to east along the valley floor and as sore as I was, after crossing the river I made it across those last few hundred yards in short order. As I drew into the end of the main street a warm wind like breath had pushed me from behind and sent needles of rain straight into me.

It had been a long three days since I left the campsite and all I wanted was food, coffee, and sleep. In any order.

The barroom grew dark enough to warrant an oil lamp. I swallowed the last of that rank pickled egg and repeated my question, looking up at the barkeep. "Where can I get a meal?"

"Try a campfire. About twenty miles in any direction but here."

I didn't recognize the voice behind me, but from the tone and the comment I knew it had to be someone wearing a tin star. I hadn't been away from civilized society long enough to forget that sarcastic tone peculiar to all men who have more false power than sense. You could find them most anywhere in cities, and out here on the frontier they are found more often than not pinned under a star.

I sighed and closed my eyes for a moment, trying to savor the already fading flavor of the beer on my tongue. It had been a long day. Hell, it had been a long week. And all I wanted was to follow it up with a hot meal. Potatoes. I am partial to a big plate of well-buttered potatoes, a goodly helping of beef gravy over the top of it all, and follow it up with a shot of rye whiskey and a cup of real coffee. Then I would sleep just fine. I didn't want to spend my money on both a room and a meal, so I opted for the meal — something I will do whenever faced with that choice. To some it might be a difficult decision. To me, a good meal will win hands-down every time. I have never had a problem grabbing sleep where and when I can.

But trouble was brewing. And it would continue to bubble. Again and again in each little town, no matter where I go. And all because I had the great good fortune to be born hard looking. I've never committed a major crime in my life of which I am aware, but this face leaves me a marked man. In every town I hear the same things — vagrancy, impeding justice, trespassing. I still don't know how they made that last charge stick, the sign behind the bar had said 'Public Drinking House'. The so-called of-

59

fenses I'd committed over the past few years were remarkably similar to each other, somewhat creative, depending on the intellect of the lawman and his motivation for getting me out of town, and above all, tiring as hell.

Out of necessity, you can imagine, I'm a fair hand with a gun. I've been alone enough in my life to get in a good bit of practice. Not that that particular skill would do me a bit of good in this situation, free of firearms as I was. I normally carried my two pistols and a rifle. However I was grateful I still had my Bowie knife. It's a constant presence on my belt. It's my most-used weapon, though I'm tempted to classify it more as a tool than something that I use to defend myself. I've split wood with it, gutted and skinned all manner of critter, stirred stew, pried slivers from my limbs, and even worked a slug out of my thigh with the tip. Yep, this knife, pound for pound, is the most useful thing I own.

My Percheron mount, Tiny Boy, should take that prize, but a man can't own a horse. Best he can do is to befriend it for a while. Tiny Boy and I had hit it off in decent fashion for about five years at that point. He got me where I needed to go and in return I got him fed and rubbed down and didn't ride him into the dirt. I hoped he had made it to this town before me with those thieves.

But right then I wasn't thinking of Tiny Boy or my knife or much of anything but the fading promise of food. Hot food. I was thinking that if the tingling feeling below my shoulder blades was right, and it hasn't failed me yet, then I might as well kiss good-bye any sweet dreams I had of a hot meal, a shot, that coffee, and a bath. No sir, something told me I wasn't going to be that lucky. As if in agreement, lightning and thunder assaulted the air again.

I opened my eyes and looked at the bartender. He'd backed down to the far end and was busy rearranging rows of upended glasses on a towel. He must have said something earlier, motioned to one of those fellas at the table off in the corner, who probably rabbited to the local lawdog. And all because I bore a remarkable likeness to no one in particular and yet to every criminal in general. It sounds unbelievable, but it's true. As sure as there are stacks of wanted sheets on a marshal's desk, as sure as bluebottle flies will settle on a fresh road apple, as sure as a grizzly will bury a fresh kill and return to it only when it's crawling with maggots, I knew I would be in jail or run out of town even before I belched the last of my beer.

It's gotten so bad at times that I don't even bother with banks anymore. The last one I entered emptied out in short order. All I wanted was to cash a pay chit from my former trail boss for services rendered and employment cut short — I'd been accused of raiding the cook's emergency stores of ready cash. It didn't matter that I was on watch amidst the longhorns when the theft took place. From then on I'd kept my money in a couple of spots about my traps, a few small gold nuggets in a slit in the cantle of my saddle.

I've been told it's a case of mistaken identity more times than 1 can remember. And I had my fill of it before I ever reached Tall Pine. So when that marshal in his roundabout way asked me to mosey on out of there when I'd just arrived, and was so close to a hot meal. . . . I turned around and looked at him, careful to not rest my elbows on the bar, careful to keep Fatso polishing his dirty glasses to my right at the edge of my sight line.

The marshal was a tall man, clean and thin with a face women would consider handsome and men would envy, for the same reason. Unlike his town, he was not ratty about the edges. And unlike the town, there was not a general air of disappointment about him. He nearly beamed at me.

"Don't I know you?" he said.

I sighed inside and wondered not for the last time if I would ever not hear that. "I doubt it, marshal. I've never been here before."

He tilted his head to the side and smirked. "I've not spent all my time in Tall Pine, you know."

Great. Next it'll be how I look an awful lot like most of the people in his little stack of dog-eared Wanted dodgers. I could see his mind working, adding up all those reward figures. Which sported the highest amount? Whichever it was, you can bet that would be me. Or I'd be him. It didn't matter anymore. I wondered if, in time, a part of me would become a bit of each of those bad men.

"Now marshal, I came in here looking for a cool glass of beer." I flicked the empty mug with my fingertip. "And I'm still looking for one. And a hot meal, maybe a bath, a soft bed to sleep in. Nothing more. Well, maybe a cup of real coffee. But that's it. I'll be on my way tomorrow. Last time I checked, these things are still well within a man's legal right and grasp, maybe even here in Tall Pine."

He stood up straighter and rested his gun hand high on his waist. He poked a finger up under his hat brim to clear his line of sight. "Are you trying to tell me the law in my own town?"

"I wouldn't dream of doing that, marshal. I'm telling you that I am thirsty and hungry and tired, though not necessarily in that order."

His mouth smiled, but his eyes didn't make it a matched set. He didn't have anything in his mouth but his tongue, but I could tell he was chewing on something. He was looking at me, through me, and see-ing something he wanted to see. An idea forming. And then the eyes smiled and he came back to himself. "How long you say you been in town, fella?"

He knew something I didn't know. "I didn't say. But now that you're asking, I just arrived. Ask our busy friend here." I nodded toward the big bartender without taking my eyes from the lawman. The big man moved further down the bar and tried to make himself more inconspicuous, an admirable but impossible task.

"I didn't see a strange horse outside."

"That's good," I said, "because if you did that would mean you're having visions.

64

Could be related to your line of work. All that responsibility would make a lesser man light-headed."

"Wise-acre, huh?"

I wish I knew when to keep my mouth shut, but I don't. Years of bearing people's blind fear and ridicule have made my tongue a reckless and troublesome creature all its own.

He shifted his stance. "So no horse, and from the looks of things you came out the loser in some sort of fight. I got that about right?"

I sighed and stared at him for a second. What the heck, I thought. It can't hurt my situation. "You won't believe me, but I'll tell you anyway. I was attacked by a bear. You see these claw marks on my face and shoulder? I killed it, but then these two outlaws jumped me and stole my horse and everything else I own."

One of the three card-playing men in the back corner shook his head and smiled, slapping down his cards. I hoped my sad story hadn't made him lose his concentration. Another one giggled low and quiet, like a whisper. I couldn't blame them. If it wasn't for my aching head and ribs, I'm not so sure I'd believe me either. Other than the drawn-out squeak of floorboards as

Fatso shifted from one foot to the other, the place was silent.

"You know, you're right," said the marshal, looking at me as if seeing me for the first time. "As it happens, I don't believe a word you just said."

I should have seen it coming, but then again lack of food and sleep have been known to dull me.

"Nope, I'm not buying." He chewed some more on something. "I'd say you been here a day at least, all right." But there was no question to it. I got the impression that it was now a fact, and that he was a man who, once he made them, didn't back away from his decisions.

And right then I counted two more things that were wrong. A brief stab of afternoon sun had sneaked through a rent in the dark storm clouds and slanted up over the tallest building across the street. It glowed through that window directly behind the marshal and right into my eyes. And the other wrong thing was Fatso. With all this talking I forgot about him. He wasn't off to my right anymore. The marshal's eyelids twitched and I knew either Fatso was going to hit me hard with something even harder or . . . ah, there it was, the unmistakable throaty clicks of shotgun hammers cocking back all the way.

I hoped he didn't have too much chicken grease on his fingers.

The marshal smiled and pulled his pistol. "Now ease that knife to the floor slow. All right?"

I drew the knife halfway from the sheath.

"Uh-uh," said the marshal, shaking his head. "You leave that sticker sheathed and take off the whole belt, all right?"

I did, managing a half-step forward at the same time. My cleverness did not go unnoticed.

"Far enough," said a fat voice behind me. I was confused. Apparently so was Fatso.

"Slim, shut your mouth. Last time I looked I wore the badge in Tall Pine, all right?"

"Do you always do that?" I asked, raising my hands slowly.

The marshal narrowed his eyes and said, "What?"

I shook my head, didn't say any more. My mouth would be the death of me yet. Prove old Maple Jack right. The floorboards popped and groaned. Fatso came around the bar.

"Pick that up," the marshal wagged his pistol at my knife and belt. Fatso stood by my side. We both looked at the marshal. Fatso hoped he meant me. I went with it and reached down.

"Not you." He wagged that pistol again. "Slim, get that belt, all right?"

The big man grunted and fumbled. He tried to hold the cocked shotgun and keep an eye on me and bend a body that had been conditioned to not bend any lower than the height of a chair seat. I have no idea how he pulled on his boots in the morning. Maybe he slept in them. He tried to slip the shotgun barrels through the belt but it kept slipping off. He finally shifted his eyes from me and laid down the shotgun. He got all the way down on his hands and knees, looking like a great sweating bear, and picked up the belt.

I waited until he was halfway up and said, "Slim?" He paused and looked at me, eyebrows raised.

"Just checking," I said.

He pulled himself up by the edge of the bar, growling and grunting the whole way. Part bear, I knew it.

I misjudged Slim. Most fat men are of an even temperament, and go out of their way to be cordial. But every once in a while life will surprise you with exceptions to every rule. I haven't yet found a way to see them coming. That's why they're called exceptions, I guess. Slim was one of the biggest

I'd come across in a long time.

Something that felt a lot like the butt end of a shotgun stock slammed into the side of my head, pinching the tip of my ear and sending a warm feeling down my face. I think I lost my hat. As that glowing sun dimmed. I heard someone say, "Well, all right, all right."

I awoke with a shock, sputtering and gasping. Someone had dumped water on me. For a second I had no idea where I was. I focused on the two men staring down at me, the fat one smiling, the taller, thinner man staring. Then I remembered it all. What a week.

"Get up," said the marshal, turning away. "We ain't gonna carry you. You can get to the jailhouse under your own steam."

I pulled myself up by the plank bar, swaying and shaking my head. I was as unsteady on my feet as I had been after fighting with the grizzly, but I returned the marshal's look. "What am I rumored to have done?" I touched the side of my head. It throbbed like I'd spent the evening with a bad bottle.

"I think everybody in this town knows what you did, all right." He looked around the room. It was then I noticed that in addition to the three gamblers standing by their table, a handful of people crowded the doorway. The afternoon had grown darker once again and the rain ran off the leaning porch roof behind the gaunt and gray people, their clothes wet and hanging off them. No expressions on their faces, they stared at me as if I was famous.

To my knowledge I'd done nothing to warrant any attention at all, especially in this little corner of hell. At that moment all I wanted was to walk out of there and keep on walking, lightning or no, right up the fifty-yard-long main street, past the dozen buildings, one of which had two stories, the rest were a cobbled-together assortment of logs and scrap lumber. Funny how a man's outlook and opinion will change when he's faced with a little hardship.

In fact, the only person in the place who seemed inclined toward smiling was the marshal. He rocked on his heels, regarding me in that same tilted-head way he had before. Then, as if he decided something, he said, "Let's go. Clear out the way, folks. Prisoner coming through. Federal marshal will be along in a few weeks. Then I suspect we'll have ourselves a hanging. Been a while, eh folks? Bring him on over to the jail, Slim."

I noticed Slim hesitate, gripping his shotgun and shifting weight to his other foot. The marshal noticed too. "Slim," he said, then turned. The marshal was a cool character who looked to be the sort in control of every setting in which he found himself. "I said to bring the prisoner to the jail."

Slim cleared his throat. "Marshal, I got to watch the bar. You know how Purly will be if —"

"Who's the marshal in these parts?"

Slim looked around. No one had the answer. He risked it. "You are, marshal."

"Just checking. Now let's go."

As we clumped to the door, the marshal plunked my hat on my head and nodded at me. I thought for sure he'd follow it up with a wink. The closer we got, the wider the gap in the little crowd grew. Reminded me of something I'd read once. Only the marshal was definitely no Moses.

I was halfway across the narrow porch and already feeling spattering rain and wind on my face when the marshal spoke up. "That's right folks, he's the one. We got 'im. It's what I'm paid for, all right." He said it as if he were talking about the weather.

Those drooping, emotionless people of seconds before closed in on me from either side. They slapped and punched at me, kicked and shouted curses. I wasn't bound and I fought back, landing a solid punch smack on the nose of one leering little man. The shouts increased, people pressed closer, and arms pummeled me. I saw enraged women, their teeth gritted and eyes squinted. I gave serious thought to fleeing into the rain and then someone landed a rib punch. I bent forward, then something hit me on my already bloody and sore head. I felt my legs weaken and buckle and I went down to my knees in front of the steps leading to the muddy street below.

The marshal's voice came to me as if through a tunnel. "All right, all right. That's enough of that. Let him be. Slim, grab hold of him. I'll take the scattergun. Drag him to the jail."

I felt strong hands grip me under my armpits and lift. I heard a grunt and then I was spun around and dragged backward down the steps. Clunk, clunk, clunk, then splash, my boots dragged, leaving little water-filled furrows behind me. The rain felt good on my face and revived me enough that I looked up.

The small crowd stared down at me from the porch, the faces blurred and ran into one another. In the back row I saw a big-hatted man blur and become two, then one again. He looked familiar. Beside him, a rounded bump. I squinted and shook my head. It was a bowler hat with a dirty face beneath it. Why would that bother me?

I heard grunting and the tugging slowed.

"Come on, Slim. Put some of your meat into it."

"He ain't light, marshal."

"Well, you're almost there, all right. Get 'im there and then you can take a breather. Now let's go."

The dragging resumed and I continued to stare at the faces as they receded in the rain. Then I knew who those faces in the back row were. I struggled and shook my head. "Marshal," I said.

Slim stopped dragging me. "He's sayin' something, marshal."

"I can hear as well as you can, Slim."

"It's them," I said, trying to point at the people. My words were muddier than the damn road. "The ones who robbed me. In the back there. Two brothers. Bowler —"

My head jerked to one side and hot pain flowered up and over my already throbbing scalp.

CHAPTER SIX

". . . Ought to give some thought to waking up, y'hear?"

It was the voice of God. Or a freight train.

An awful clanging joined the voice that was saying, "Hey! Hey you!"

God on a train. I opened my eyes and that took all my strength. The sun stared down on me. I took it as a good sign and turned my head to find out what God riding a freight train looked like. I have to say I was disappointed. An old man with no teeth, a chaw-stained beard, and a flop-brim hat smiled through steel bars at me. He dragged a tin cup across the bars and said, "Mornin'." What was God doing behind bars?

I answered, but no one told me that I could speak Latin so fluently.

"Come again?" said God.

I pushed myself up to a sitting position and the earth swayed and lifted before settling down to a more reasonable version of itself. I touched my head and wished I hadn't. That side was swollen and there was something split and rubbery stuck to it that once could have been my ear.

"You took a wallopin'. Course, you mighta deserved it." God shuffled off and it occurred to me that he wasn't behind the bars. He was in front of them.

I tried English again. "What . . ." I swallowed. "What do you mean?"

He turned back and the tin cup was full of something hot and steaming. He held it toward me. "You're gonna have to get up and take this. I wouldn't wait on ya even if I had keys."

As much as I wanted to sit still I could smell that was real coffee and I figured that only a dead man would ignore that heavenly scent, so I pushed to my feet. A lifetime later I had that cup in my hands, so hot it burned my fingers. I let it. It helped to clear the cotton batting from my head. I even let it burn my mouth. Never had a mouthful of anything tasted so good.

"You look pretty bad." He was staring at me.

"Thanks."

"I'll get you some water. Clean yourself up."

While he was gone I drank my coffee and tried not to think of what I didn't do to deserve these accommodations. He returned with a shallow pan slopping full of steaming hot water. An old piece of white flannel floated in it. He slid it under the door through the wide space in the bars meant for food trays. I was familiar with this feature.

"What did you mean when you said that I deserved this?" I said as I dabbed at my swollen head.

He carved a thick, black curl of tobacco off a lint-covered block. If I had eaten much the day before, I would have had that to deal with as well. There's always an upside to starving.

"Well now, I could get myself in trouble for sayin' too much. But I ain't never found trouble by keeping my mouth shut." He looked at me as if waiting for a response.

"Fair enough," I finally said. By now the water in the pan was a deep red, almost black. I looked out the window and found myself at the end of Tall Pine's main street. Something plinked off the wall to the left of the window. A handful of men, a couple of women, and some children stared at the jailhouse from thirty feet away. They were shouting and a few of them arched their arms. A rock made it in through the barred window and pinged off the cell door. The old man, who by now I was pretty sure wasn't God, stepped back and kept chewing.

He laughed. "You're not popular here, mister."

"I wonder why that is," I said, and I meant it.

He stopped chewing, his cheek bulging with the chaw. "If you really don't know then you're either mighty forgetful or a liar."

"Or innocent," I said, assuming the worst. "This has something to do with that marshal, doesn't it?"

"Doesn't everything in this town?" He mumbled it, but I heard him. He turned back to his table and held up the coffee pot. I passed him my cup. As he filled it he said, "The child died in the night."

He wasn't making sense. In fact, none of this made sense, but I was curious now. "What child are you talking about?"

He moved close to the bars and held the cup through. As I took it, he held it and stared into my face. "Young James Dougal was beat pretty bad and close to strangled two days back. Whoever did it left him for dead."

There was a long pause. Finally I said,

"He lived then. For a while."

The old man let go of the cup but still stared at me. "Yep. He didn't come around, though. Too bad. . . ."

The awful weight of his words, the meaning behind them, occurred to me then. "So people here think I killed him? A child?"

He didn't say anything, but stared at me.

"But surely people saw me walk into town yesterday. It was yesterday when they brought me in here, right?"

"Yep, it was yesterday."

The incidents of the previous day came back to me — the crowd on the barroom steps, the rain, the mud . . . and the faces of the two thieves.

My thoughts were interrupted by the clunking of boots off to the left, out of my sight line. But from the tightening of the old man's features, I guessed his boss had arrived even before I heard that nasally voice from yesterday's saloon get-together.

"What are you doin', Finchy?"

The old man turned to the table and gathered up the coffee pot. "Bringing the prisoner coffee is all. Like I always do."

The marshal came into view, smiling and not looking at me yet. Finchy edged by the marshal, who didn't move out of his way, arms still spread, hands on his hips. As

78

Finchy shuffled out of view I heard him say, "I reckon breakfast'll be here shortly."

The marshal turned to face me now, still smiling, and said, "Not for this one." He smiled wider, still staring at me. "But I sure am hungry. Mmm-hmm. Catching killers is hungry-making work."

If I thought I had a chance of getting away with it I would have reached through the bars and choked him. And that put the dead boy in my mind. It hadn't been me who'd killed him, but how easy it could be to kill a person. I hadn't had to kill a man in a long time, but that didn't mean that I hadn't felt like dealing the final blow to a few folks over the years. And this fellow came as close as anyone to receiving my full hate at that very moment. I was in here because of him, it was pushing two days since I'd eaten, and my head felt twice the size it should have been.

"You ain't gonna let him eat?"

The marshal turned to Finchy and said, "I think you heard what I said, all right." He turned back to me. "How's that sit with you, child killer?"

"I didn't kill anybody, let alone a child. But then you knew that."

My words hung in the air between us. He stared at me with no expression. I decided to take advantage of the fact that I had nothing to lose. "Tell me," I said, leaning closer to the bars. "How does a marshal such as yourself come to protect thieves? Or is that normal in this town?"

Suddenly he looked old and haggard. And I knew I had struck a nerve. Somehow, somewhere I got to him. But only for a moment. That damnable smug smile crept back onto his mouth and he said, "You got a visitor, killer man."

He walked to the door. I heard it creak open and he said in a loud voice, "Come on in, sweetheart."

A softer step sounded on the wood floor and then I heard a woman's flat voice say, "Get away from me."

I heard his voice, an insistent near-whisper, say, "You're making it hard on yourself, darlin'. If you was to marry me, why you could be queen of this town, all right."

Heartless, handsome, and bold, I thought.

She did not respond to him.

The door squeaked and the marshal stepped back, just into my view, still wearing that self-confident smile. She came into sight before she saw me and pulled away from the marshal's grip on her arm. She hugged her arms close but didn't look at him. Loose strands of hair hung in her face. He stared at her, his smile fading. They walked to my cell door and she still didn't look up. He stood there with his arms crossed, then winked at me. "I'll leave you to it, all right."

Then he turned and brushed against her enough to push her closer to the cell. All I could see was her unkempt hair, gray streaking dark brown, her arms folded tight across her belly. Her dress was dirty, and looked as though she hadn't changed in days. The door squeaked, boots clunked slowly down what must have been a hallway, and then she lifted her head and looked at me.

I am not a skittish man by nature. I've been surprised any number of times by loud-mouth drunks with guns who thought I looked up to the task and I've always stood my ground. I've been bushwhacked by a down-on-his-luck miner who it turned out had the same name as someone I knew from my childhood, though it was not the same person. But nothing prepared me for this woman.

As soon as I saw her face, I knew who it was. Those aged eyes rimmed red and cried out, her nose as red, the mouth set straight across like a rail fence blocking entrance.

This was the dead boy's mother. Even though there were bars between us I took a step backward. I couldn't help it.

And now that she was no longer in shadow, I saw that one eye wore a violet smudge underneath, high on her cheekbone, as if she were overtired half the time. "Why did you kill my boy?"

I expected the question, or worse, but it still felt as though I had been gut-unched hard while smiling. Of all the questions a man could be on the receiving end of, that has to be the most difficult. How does a man go about answering that?

I gained back my step and she stood right there, inches from the bars, inches from my hands, and I looked her in the eye and said, "Someone had to have a reason to do something like that, however wrong it might be. I am truly sorry to hear of your loss, but I had nothing to do with it. I don't even know anybody in this town. I arrived yesterday afternoon looking for a hot meal."

She stared back at me for a few moments more then exhaled quickly, a shuddering sound, as if she was reluctant to let go of each little second of breath. Her eyes told me she had decided something. I think she knew before she came to see me. But she was a woman who no longer trusted her instincts.

The day was already shaping up to be one of those humid, sunny affairs where your clothes cling to you and sweat runs down your back. Mud from the previous day's rainstorm puckered and curled in the lane outside my cell window. The shouts of the crowd outside rose and fell according to the amount of hot air available. I guessed that today they would have a steady supply.

"I know who did it," she said in a voice little more than a whisper, as if she had known all along. "But I don't know why. . . ."

"Ma'am," I said, grabbing the bars. She didn't move. "If you're convinced I didn't do it, I'd appreciate it if you'd tell the marshal so I don't hang." And even as I said it I saw the change in her eyes. It was a subtle shift. In less time than it takes to blink, the fear and look of defeat replaced that momentary flare of conviction of seconds before. And then I, too, knew who killed her son. And I knew that I would probably hang for the crime anyway.

But I was a long way from dead. Another rock whanged against the iron bars of the window. "Ma'am, who hit your face —"

But she interrupted. "I know what to do now." She turned toward the door. I told

83

her to be careful. She stopped and I thought she might turn around, but she continued on through the door, her shoes clunking against the wood.

I leaned against the wall by the window and peeked through. For the moment the crowd lost interest in my window. It grew silent and a few seconds later the rabble parted ranks and she walked right through the middle of them. She disappeared between two buildings at the far end of the street and they stared after her. So did I.

CHAPTER SEVEN

It felt as though it should have been dark, but since it was nearly summer time I knew it was late in the day. I still hadn't eaten anything. At some point I realized that my coin purse was missing from around my neck. Not surprising. I would have been more surprised if it had still been with me.

Several times during the day, when I thought I heard footsteps in the marshal's office down that hallway, I yelled for water, food, anything. But when I raised my voice my head throbbed like a cannon volley. I thought of yelling out the window, but I reasoned that a food request from someone who was considered prime lynching material might not endear me to the sputtering mob.

I was too tired, hungry, and sore to give much thought to the problem at hand, but when my thoughts drifted to food and sleep and pain-free living, I forced myself to think of the consequences of not doing anything and that scared me enough to think harder.

I didn't have much to work with, but I knew somehow that the marshal was guilty of murder. Why? I had no idea. I saw how he treated her and I saw how she took it — well, considering her predicament. I also saw the look of pain and defeat in her eyes and that would probably cloud out everything else in the end.

No matter what the dime novels tell us, good folks don't always get the upper hand. It's the powerful who usually win out in the end. It works that way in nature. Who is man to think it's any different than wolves in a pack or elk in a herd or crows in a flock? If the marshal killed the boy and she knows it, then the marshal has some sort of power over her. Something sinister and unspoken.

I thought back on her eyes. For a moment I had seen the glint of something that might get me freed or might get her in trouble. The worst kind of trouble. The kind you don't recover from. But with her son dead, did she care anymore what might happen to her?

I finally gave up and laid back on the roughest cot I have ever been acquainted with. I must have been bone tired because the next thing I knew it was dark and I woke up in heaven. The smell of coffee and chicken and rolls and butter and berry pie lifted me up off that cot as if I had angel wings.

"Hope you're hungry, boy, 'cause Mother's outdone herself tonight. I already et, so I know."

Finchy's back was to me as he stood over his little hall table. An oil lantern glowed enough to let me see the golden skin of chicken, steam from a cup of coffee, and I fancy I saw a pat of butter losing a fight with that warm browned roll. He handed the coffee through to me and I set it on the edge of the bunk. He turned back to the table and had lifted the tin plate by the edges — I was already opening my mouth like a baby bird — when a shadow moved between the cell door and Finchy, crossed the glow of the lamp, and I heard a dull thunking sound. Finchy fell forward, hit the little table, and slipped to the floor. Food and tinware flew into the air and the table's contents landed all over him. It seemed like a joke or a bad dream.

Then a voice said, "If I told him once, it was a hundred times. He was not to feed this prisoner. He'll never learn." The marshal stepped into the lamp glow and said, "You know what, drifter? We ain't gonna wait for the federal marshal. We're gonna do this by my rules. I'm a fair man, just ask anybody in this town, all right, and they'll tell you true." He smiled and pulled a ring of keys from his back pocket, jangled them in front of his face, and unlocked the cell door. Then he tossed the keys on the floor by Finchy's sprawled body and stepped back from the door.

"Come on," he said.

"No." I stood still in the center of the cell. "You're up to something and I don't want any part of it. There's still someone who knows I am innocent, besides you. I'm better off waiting right here." I was bluffing far beyond the value of anything I had and my stomach knew it.

"So sure of yourself, smart mouth. Well don't be." He pulled his pistol and cocked the hammer. "Let's go." He gestured with the pistol. Despite a man's convictions, there are certain things he'd do better to not disobey, and number one on that list is a heartless man with a gun. I swung open the door. As I stepped into the hallway in the dim, fluttering light of the oil lantern I saw welts on the marshal's lips, and what looked like scratches on his chin.

"Tangle with a mountain lion, marshal?"

He came up behind me fast. I could smell

88

his rank, nervous sweat. He kicked me behind the knees and I fell forward, tripping over Finchy's legs. I was weak and my arms didn't prevent my face from hitting the wood floor. This time the other side of my head was ringing. Perfect, a matched set. I opened my eyes and a big, juicy chicken leg was so close I could have licked it. I know because I tried. As I stood up I grabbed it and raised it to my mouth. Of course, he knocked it from my hand.

"No, no, no," he said. "How many times do I have to tell you, all right?"

I stood there too weak to argue, my head hanging down, my arms limp.

"Keep walking, killer man. Straight ahead."

I looked into the dark ahead of me. "Doorway's over there," I said.

"This is the back way. Now move."

I walked, feeling my way in the near black. Light from the moon angled in through a small barred window.

"To your right," he said and pushed me into a door that swung open as I touched it. We were in the back alley. A horse nickered ahead of me in the dark. "Now, get on that horse and run, child killer. Be a few hours before the posse catches up with you. But it will."

To say I was confused would be understating my situation. But I pulled myself into the saddle just the same. It wasn't my horse, but it felt like a sturdy mount and saddle. I groped for a sheathed rifle, knife, anything, but no luck.

"Now git," he said, "before I change my mind and kill you right now." He laughed and I urged the horse into a trot with my heels. I laid low over the pommel, trying to reduce myself as a target. I expected a bullet in the back any second. He would be justified in the townsfolk's eyes to shoot me now and claim I was escaping.

I didn't have much idea what was going on, but pieces were coming together. The cool air of the evening felt good after the stale air and sweat stink of the jail cell. Except for the heavenly scent of the food Finchy'd brought, that is. I was still imagining what that chicken would have tasted like as I broke that horse into a gallop west out of town, hoping the kindly old man hadn't been hit too hard by the damnable marshal.

CHAPTER EIGHT

I have tracked men and I have been tracked and neither one is a pleasant experience, I can tell you. When you're on someone's trail you're afraid they might pop up behind every boulder you ride up on and catch you dead to rights. And if you're being followed you imagine every deadfall hides someone hoping to claim their share of the bounty, be it glory or revenge or money. Before I spotted the morning's first light I slowed and looked for a place to hole up.

The hills in these parts are gradual and rolling and only sparsely treed. I reasoned that if I could find a place well into the undergrowth I might be able to wait out the posse. As I picked my way among a tumble-down of boulders at the base of a ragged little peak, I went over in my mind for the fiftieth time that night what the marshal's motives might be in letting me go. He was covering up something, that much was certain. The welts and scratches on his face told part of the story, but which part was anybody's guess.

All night I had reasoned without success about why the marshal set me free. If he wanted to further fix the idea of my guilt in the townspeople's minds, then he could do worse than to stage an escape, pinning Finchy's braining on me, and probably theft of the horse I rode hard all night, too. But why did he let me go? Why not shoot me in the back as I rode away and claim he got there too late to prevent the breakout and help Finchy, but not too late to stop me from getting away? That is the point where time and again through the night's hard riding I came up against those dueling twin faces of reason: bare fact and raw speculation.

I was so tired that I could barely keep my eyes open. Any surge of power I may have gained from being freed in such a bizarre manner was long gone, even the tail end of its momentum had long abated. The horse, a fine bay with a good set of legs under him and a tooled saddle on top of him, felt the same. He was flagging. We needed water and rest and the best source for both would be deeper into these treed slopes to the north.

The big bay found water. Always trust a horse's nose. I let him follow it and soon we were drinking from a small, clear stream that bubbled its way through the thickening forest. I bathed my sore head — it seemed one part or another of me had been sore my entire life.

We picked a path deeper into the foothills where spruce, poplar, and birch grew tall and a breeze played the leaves, offering a sound like ocean waves washing over sand. And for a few minutes I was carefree again, breathing in crisp morning air, and feeling the random shafts of warming, restorative sun filtered through the treetops. The bay's steps were lighter, he snorted and sniffed at the breeze, and shook his head from time to time.

I found a low, hollowed spot thick with trees, save for a patch of wispy grass large enough to keep the horse busy, if not satisfied, for a few hours. I hobbled him with a length of rein leather and hoped it would hold him close by. Keeping him quiet was another matter. If he heard other horses he was inclined to nicker and that would reveal my position. I had taken pains to backtrail and wipe out what traces I could of our presence, especially closer to our hiding place.

Though the water went a long way in restoring my strength, hunger gnawed at my insides like it would soon poke through to my outsides. After I took care of the horse I flopped to my knees in the grass and rooted for anything that might give sustenance. I couldn't find any early berries and I didn't dare venture beyond our hiding place to search further.

I pulled up a stringy white root that tasted so bitter I spat it out and wiped my mouth on my grimy shirt. I finally settled for lichen that I scraped off a boulder, and forced myself to chew a handful of short grass. It was sweeter close to the root, which explained the bay's continued interest in it. And though it was hardly satisfying, it was something in my gut. I ended up chewing on some bark for the sheer pleasure of using my mouth for something more than mumbling complaints. Then I found a spot in undergrowth against the slope and piled more deadfall branches and leaves into what I hoped was a natural-looking little shelter. Then I settled in for a bit of rest while I could get it.

A normal man in the trouble I was in

might have been inclined to run that horse ragged in any direction but back to Tall Pine. But I guess I'm not normal, because while I lay there I was thinking of what I might do to get things righted. Go back to that town? Certain death. Wait until dark and head out on the run? Greater possibility of survival but it meant a life on the run. The limitations of these possibilities repeated themselves with no solution halting the cycle. And so was my state of mind when sleep finally pulled me down.

The bay nickered low and I awoke fully, curled up behind my brush pile. I heard something clumping the earth, then the sound doubled. Two horses? And close enough for me to hear. I cursed myself for using old leaves. They rustled with every move I made. The sound faded and as it did I fancy I heard a man's voice, though I couldn't make out the words. I listened a moment more and as quietly as I could I slid myself, pulling with my elbows, out of my resting spot. Crouching, I ran over to the horse.

"Good old boy," I told him and rubbed under his neck and jaw. I was surprised that the two horses that passed hadn't indicated to their riders that there was a strange horse nearby. They probably tried, but a man must be sensitive to his horse. As I untied the hobble and rerigged the reins, I kept a sharp ear and sure enough those two riders retraced their steps, but this time came down the other side of our hidden glade.

And this time I did hear a voice, then another. Had I heard those voices before? In town? Difficult to tell, though they may have had an edge of familiarity about them. The bay lifted his head and perked his ears. I scratched between his eyes and whispered low to him.

". . . too much. I'm all for headin' back," said the first voice.

A second voice, deeper, broke in and said, "We can't just give up and you know it. That man killed a boy and the boy's mother and stole a horse. We can't let that stand."

I froze. This was news I had not anticipated. Bad news.

"And don't forget Finchy," said the first voice, a younger man.

"He took quite a knock. But that old dog is tough as nails."

"Yeh. Marshal's taking all this pretty hard, though."

"Well, that was his girl. Or at least he wanted it that way. Not so sure she felt the same way."

"We'll never know."

"You reckon the marshal was serious when he said we could go ahead and either shoot or drag them other two fellas back in? Seemed all right to me."

"Marshal is a serious man when it comes to money. I know that — still claims I overcharged him for digging Big Burl's grave."

"Damn, that's right. Woman lost her husband, then her son, and then she up and gets killed."

"Right enough. Some families is just that way. But if he's offering a reward, then that's reason enough for me to plug a few bandits."

"Hell, you ain't never shot nobody."

"Have to."

"Ain't neither."

"Well, neither have you."

One of them dismounted.

"What are you doing?"

There was a pause, then a sound like rain on leaves. "What's it look like?"

"Hurry up, then."

The bay jerked his head up and down. I laid a firm hand on his muzzle, and had to rub his throat hard to distract him. The man remounted but they didn't ride on. There were small sounds, shiftings in the saddle, something crinkled. Then I heard a match flare and it wasn't too long after that I recognized the pinched odor of tobacco smoke. It always smells out of place outdoors. Nothing I could ever get used to. I'd tried, but smoking wasn't for me. Not for the bay, either. He nickered low and I had a time to keep him from moving his feet.

"You hear that?" It was the deeper voice.

A pause, then "Nope."

"All right, we better find the others. If you're done, that is. My word, you're worse than a woman with all your fussin'."

"That'll be enough from you," said the younger man in a deep, mocking tone, then they both laughed and soon all that was left of their presence was the fading smell of cigarette smoke. That and the information they'd given me. That poor woman had already been through so much. Much more, I realized, than the murder of her son. I remembered her tired eyes and all that gray in her limp brown hair. And now she, too, was dead.

I stood there, leaning against the drowsy bay, patting and scratching his neck and spending the time reasoning out what I knew. So it seemed the marshal had put a price on the thieves' heads. Under normal circumstances I would not be bothered by that news, but today I had a problem with it. They were my alibi. And they were the only way I could prove my innocence to the townspeople — for proving it to the marshal would be a waste of time since it was obvious, at least to me, that he was the guilty party. But how to convince the townsfolk of this?

Call the information from those two posse members a lucky break, call it divine intervention, I don't care what label it carried, but as they rode off I knew what I had to do. I was not about to let that marshal get away with murder and saddle me with the blame. And he would get away with it if anything happened to those thieves. My best chance at clearing up this mess was for me to convince them that the marshal was using them.

The marshal was no doubt hoping his posse might kill the two renegades who happened to show up in the wrong town at the wrong time. But would he trust that the renegades wouldn't talk in front of the townsfolk? Probably not. So what would he most likely do?

He would most likely take care of them himself. He wasn't so worried about me because I was already a proven killer in the eyes of the townsfolk. But those two outlaws had most likely frittered a good deal of time in the town, spending money and generally filling the coffers, at least to a certain extent, better than anyone had in a long time. Their guilt would be a harder sell than mine. But their deaths, if they involved money, would be accepted. So how was he going to take care of them?

The thought occurred to me and I took a deep breath, knowing what it would entail on my part, and I nodded my head slowly to no one in particular. It was going to be a long day and night. I couldn't leave my hiding spot and yet I had no time to waste.

It was all I could do to keep from mounting up and riding as fast as that horse would carry me back to town. But a hasty act like that would only serve to get me killed without ever seeing the marshal. I had no weapons, but I did have a tired horse and fifteen miles to go in broad daylight. No, it was better to bide my time. I would work my way back to Tall Pine and sneak into town at dark. I spent the next twelve seconds trying to figure out details of this master plan, but it was a waste of effort. I needed a weapon and I knew where to get one. It would require a break-in. Beyond that, I had no idea what to do.

The marshal might be at the jailhouse,

considering he'd clubbed his overnight help in the head. That was my plan, then. Ride into town, steal a gun, and knock on the jailhouse door? Too complex. I scraped more lichen, waited for dark, and thought some more. What I really needed was to get to the thieves before the marshal did. Because if he beat me to it, they'd be dead. And they were my only alibi. I'd need every advantage I could give myself. I vowed I would make that marshal talk or I would die trying. Before tomorrow morning, I thought, I would either be free or be dead.

I took the two posse members' less-than-interested attitude to mean that if I was careful I could start back right away, if I stuck to the hills north of town and so probably north of any stray-but-dedicated posse members. This would land me back in town after dark, as I wanted it. We rode upslope, rustling and crunching too much for my taste through the leaves and twigs as the afternoon sun dappled the still-new, vivid green canopy overhead. I kept the bay at a slow pace, remaining hidden whenever possible. I hunched low in the saddle and after a half-hour I reined us east. I reasoned that would eventually put us even with the town, though a few miles to the north. It was a risky route, but I would be well hidden in the forested hills.

With a dedicated direction for a few hours, my thoughts turned back to speculating about the marshal's next move. If my guess was correct he would have sent the two thieves off in a different direction than the one he sent me and the posse. Once the posse was safely away from town and doing its untrained best to dog my trail, then the marshal would be free to take off after the two outlaws and dispense with them far away from prying eyes. I doubt there was any state or federal reward for them, of course. That was a fabrication on the marshal's part, something to sweeten the pot and help raise the posse's blood to a slow boil and instigate interest among the men of the town in the dangerous work of tracking fugitives.

I was also pretty sure that the marshal would do what he could to keep them close at hand. I know I would if I found myself in his position. I shifted in my saddle. The flaws in my plan were plenty. There was nothing saying the thieves would do as the marshal suggested, or even that the marshal suggested such a plan to them. Though he guessed that they would like to see me dead, as it would take any of the blame of their theft of Tiny Boy and my gear off them.

It seemed like the sort of logical plan the marshal might use. And logic, I told myself, was the cold-blooded killer's preferred mode of operation.

Also, it was a long distance for a tired horse and man to travel, though our brief rest would have to suffice in renewing our energy stores. I might also get there too late to prevent the marshal from killing my only alibis, the very men who had robbed me and left me to live or die in the wilderness but a few days before. Those same men for whom I wished nothing but ill fortune then, I now wished all manner of good luck and safety. The irony of my situation gripped me with a sudden enthusiasm to ensure that my plan — or lack of it — succeeded. I put heels to the bay's belly and we charged northeast.

I was relieved to once again force something to happen. I have never been one to wait for events in life to happen to me, and the further I rode toward Tall Pine the tighter the muscles in my throat and shoulders felt. It was a long shot but I had little to lose and all to gain. It won out, hands-down, over fleeing into the hills and always looking over my shoulder, flinching at the slightest sound and knowing that I left a murderer free to ply his vicious trade.

I'd like to say that my long shot paid off. But I'd be lying. I underestimated the marshal.

CHAPTER NINE

Progress was slow and I found myself looking behind us toward the west, wishing it
was later in the day than it actually was. It
was a futile effort but I looked back at the
sun, still hours from setting, and urged its
fiery mass to get on with the job and give
way to dark already. I silently cursed the
daylight but knew it would be a fool's er-
rand to slip into town unarmed and without
the benefit of at least the dark of nighttime,
that great leveler. We were on a tree-
shrouded route a few hundred yards south
of the crest of the ridge and the bay tensed
as I faced forward again.

Not ten yards ahead, directly in our path
and angled nearly broadside to us, sat the
marshal on a gleaming chestnut. His crisp
fawn hat was pushed back, the brim angled
high, and a wide smile spread across his
face. There were those marks on his lips and
three red welts by his mouth, evidence of

the woman's last desperate attempt at survival before he killed her the night before.

His left hand rested on the saddle horn and laid across his forearm was a Henry repeater, leveled right at me. If my surprise showed on my face, the marshal was a cool enough character that he didn't mention it. In fact, if I didn't know better I'd think he was taking in the air on a pleasure ride.

"I tell you what," he said. "It is so very fine to feel that afternoon sun after a long, cold winter and a long, wet spring."

I reined up hard and took care to face him dead on, but placing the mass of the bay's chest between us, and I angled myself slightly to one side in an effort to reduce the size of my body as a target, though these things I did more out of instinct than plan. I cut my eyes to the downhill slope. Could I plunge into that thickly treed descent before he drew on me? He answered my question for me.

"I guess I wouldn't do that if I was you, all right."

And he was right. Even if I could make it between the aspens and small scrub pines whose closeness had moments before represented a security to me, but now felt too confining, he would have a clear shot at me for more than a hundred yards even as the bay would do his best to navigate by scrambling. Yes sir, the marshal chose the spot for his ambush well.

I sat the bay and waited.

"You really could have disappointed me, child killer, but you didn't. You came right along here, as I hoped you might. It's good of you. Rarely will people do what you expect nowadays."

"Never were truer words spoken," I said, cursing myself for thinking that events would unspool as I wished them to. My frustration must have showed on my face because he laughed as though I had told him a real thigh slapper. He stopped abruptly and looked at me, half a smile still on his face. "Why, you look plain surprised to see me. I bet you want to know how I come on you like this."

He poked a finger at his hat brim and pushed it back even further. From this distance he looked like a young farm buck without a care in the world. "I'll tell you, child killer. I was settin' in that office of mine, sipping coffee and eating a plate of hot beefsteak and potatoes with gravy — good, too, for a change. I almost finished it all."

He paused and those eyes stared right into mine, then he smiled and broke the spell. I was hungrier than I'd been in years and he knew it only too well.

"So where was I? Oh yes, I ate that big ol' dinner and that's when Roberts come in. He's the haircutter, but a good man just the same. Him and the boys come back empty handed, gave up on the posse work looking for you. So I give them all a few dollars for the saloon from a little coin purse I had hanging around —"

He winked at me and I felt my face redden. My jaw tightened and I wanted to club him. But I knew that any sudden movement out of my saddle and he'd gun me down. The thread holding me to life was a short and weak one. He didn't really need to keep me alive and we both knew it. Hadn't needed to set me loose last night, either. It occurred to me that part of him enjoyed this game. Maybe even needed it.

"And then I commenced to thinking. And you know what I thought up?"

I stared at him. It was apparent he wasn't going to continue until I replied. I twitched my head and raised an eyebrow. It satisfied him.

"I thought to myself that this child killer is a clever enough fella. Why, I thought, he'd probably try to ride back to town to deal with the situation himself because he ain't the sort to live life looking back over his shoulder, all right."

He sat there grinning at me, his eyes half-closed as if he were about to doze off. "And it looks like I was right."

I shifted in the saddle and stretched my back. "Let's get one thing straight, marshal."

He lost half of the smile. "I'm all ears."

"Why don't we drop the child killer name you keep trying to saddle me with and I'll stop thinking of you as a real marshal."

The rest of the smile vanished and those mirthful eyes turned to black lake ice. "Let's go." He wagged the rifle up the trail past him.

I nudged the bay forward, closing the gap between us as slow as I could, buying precious seconds for no other reason than for the hope that during one of them I might actually come up with a better plan than the one I didn't have. It didn't work.

He had walked the chestnut to the side, the rifle cocked and trained on the middle of me. My gut muscles tightened instinctively and any thoughts I had of a sidelong attack skittered away. I was shot once at close range on a battlefield in Ohio and I had no desire to repeat the experience. I vowed to keep what was left of me with me. At least for a while longer.

"So where are you taking me?" I looked at him over my shoulder, moving slowly so I didn't startle him.

"Ride, killer."

I rode. Half an hour later I said, "So, marshal. What have you done about the men who robbed me? I alerted you to the crime committed and you promptly hit me on the head."

"Well whatever are you on about, killer?"

"I think you and I both know who I'm talking about. And we know why we're each so interested in those men."

There was a pause and while I didn't dare look back, I could have sworn that he was scowling at my shoulders. And then, as if I were watching him, I could see that damn smile spread across his face. "Oh, surely you don't mean them two crusty fellas come into town a few days back? Why, you won't believe this, but they've been asking about you, too. So much so that I thought I'd accommodate them fellas and bring you to them. Sort of a goodwill gesture, you might say."

And that's when the last piece slipped into place. As I said before, I'm not at my best when my stomach's protesting louder than an ungreased coach axle in dusty country. I cut to the chase. "What makes you think they won't get wind of your plan, that it's a little suspicious you being so nice and all, and suspect something's up? And then try to get the drop on you, marshal?" I was trying to rattle him. It didn't work. But his next statement rattled me.

"Well now I don't know about all that fancy talk. I'm a simple, small-town marshal, but I reckon if I shot all of you I'd be doing the countryside some good and saving the taxpayers some money, too. Yep, I reckon that's the thing to do. You said so yourself that they're thieves. And we know you're a killer. So it'll look like all the thieves and killers kill all the thieves and killers. Nice and neat. Then I'll get the posse to ride out that direction tomorrow and they'll find a mess and that will be that."

"Just like that." I looked over my shoulder at him, sickened but not in the least shocked by the mixing of his matter-of-fact tone and savage nature.

"Just like that, all right." He winked and nodded at me, a drowsy, satisfied look in his eyes.

It's amazing how slowly time passes when there's someone trailing a few yards behind you with a cocked rifle aimed at your back. I was so sore and tired and thirsty and hungry, and I could tell that the bay was feeling the effects of our travels, that miles back I gave up on probing the marshal for information. And really, there wasn't much more I could learn from him. He'd been an open book regarding his plans.

We passed well above Tall Pine with little more than the marshal's comments about how lovely his town looked from up on the ridge. I allowed as how the town was lucky to have such a caring marshal.

"Yes, I do believe you're right, killer."

"Too bad he won't be there much longer."

There was that pause again. I could almost predict it by now. Hit him with a raw comment and he pauses. Then he speaks.

"That's not the way I hear tell, killer."

I let it hang in the air. It wasn't much, but it was what I could do to him. At least for now.

We rode in silence for another few minutes, descending a slight grade that curved between a halved boulder as big as a house, split by mighty lightning who knows how long ago. During the trip, I had looked for any slight opportunity that might get me away from his line of fire long enough to give me a fighting chance in the scraggly forest growth. I found none that suited my situation, namely the bay's weakened condition, my identical condition, and the fact that my traveling companion had a variety of weapons on his person and he was where I couldn't see him.

Despite my problems, as the trail curved and widened, I almost enjoyed myself, as I always did in the great out-of-doors. We slowed to a saunter and the sun was blocked behind the higher ridge to our backs. The air turned cool and the light began its daily surrender to purple shadows. The marshal's voice cracked the silence of the waning afternoon.

"Better get ready, killer. Almost time to meet your maker. But first you gonna meet some old friends."

We rounded another cluster of boulders and the two thieving brothers sat right there in front of me astride their horses. Grimy the Younger showed off his dirty face and stumpy teeth in a leer under his battered bowler. His brother, under his tall, wide-brim hat, stared at me. I don't know why I was surprised.

CHAPTER TEN

"Why, hello boys! Fancy meeting you out here." The marshal's boisterous voice filled the little clearing. "Say, I believe you all have met, but let me introduce you just the same."

He rode up within my sightline on my right, his rifle once again leveled across his forearm and angled in the general center of the three of us. Clever lad, this marshal. He had us all covered and from what I could see these two thieves hadn't even drawn their sidearms.

"Fancy, hell. You sent us out here. And now I'm glad you did." Grimy squinted and continued, "Can't help wondering why you're doing the job for us, marshal?"

From his speedy response it seemed as if the marshal had anticipated this question. He shifted a little in the saddle, though I noticed the gun and forearm stayed fixed on that kill point we three shared.

"Well now, after the posse come back I got to thinking, and I guessed where this here killer might be. It come down to what it always comes down to — if I wanted the job done right I should have done it myself. I thought that if I was right, someone other than the well meaning but lazy members of my community posse should get to share in the rewards offered by the territory for this here killer. Then I saw you two and I know you're a working pair, bound to move on soon. So I thought to myself, 'Now marshal, wouldn't that teach them lazy townsfolk a good little lesson. If you bring this here outlaw in then nobody gets the reward money. And that's a shame.' Might as well share it a bit, spread the wealth."

He was a clever one, I'll give him that. He was appealing to the greed and stupidity of Grimy, the apparent spokesman for the pair. I wondered if he thought this also entitled him to do the thinking for the pair.

"You'd do that for us?"

The light was leaving, but not enough yet so that I couldn't see the look of caution and distrust the silent brother offered Grimy. The marshal saw it, too.

"Like I said, in an odd way it'd be a favor to me as the marshal. Besides, it's never a bad thing to have a lawman beholden to you, now is it?" He winked and scanned all three of us. "I'm afraid I can't let you think on it too deep. You understand I can't turn this killer over to you then leave. Not only would that be putting you innocent citizens in harm's way but it'd be releasing a known child-killer from my jurisdiction." He shifted slightly in his saddle, the gun not moving. "I have to get back to my town, duty calls. I hope you'll accompany me on the ride. We can talk about your reward money."

"Is it a lot?" Grimy was a hooked trout by this time, but his brother had managed to angle his horse the slightest bit from his full-on exposure to the marshal's rifle. I had to assume that the marshal saw the maneuver. That was good for me as it showed doubt in at least one of them. Whether it was the one who could make a difference I didn't know. It was up to me to drive a wedge into that crack of doubt until the thing split wide open.

Without waiting for the marshal's reply, I said, "Ask yourselves this, gentlemen: Has a lawman ever gone out of his way to help you?"

"You," said Grimy, turning dark eyes on me. "Keep your mouth shut. I should of kilt you when we pilfered you four, five days back —"

The silence that fell on us matched the cold surprise on Grimy's face. It only lasted seconds but in that time I swear the shadows lengthened and all the faces around me disappeared but for their eyes, those mirrors of the soul — a phrase I recalled from a book.

The marshal's smile was wider than I remember it being all afternoon. Could have been the shadows of the day's last light. Could have been that he felt the time had come for him to put the final phase of his plan into action. In fact, I believe that was his plan all along.

"Marshal?" said Grimy in a slow, measured tone. I could see the hand closest to his brother slipping, inch by inch, across his leg toward his pistol. If I was a betting man, I'd say the marshal saw it, too.

"What can I do for you?"

"What day did you say that boy was kilt?"

"Why, as a matter of fact, now that you mention it, I believe it was four, five days ago. Yes, that's it, all right."

I spoke up: "The marshal knows that when you were robbing me five days ago you gave me the watertight alibi for the killing of the young boy. There was no way I could have done the killing and he knows it."

"What about —" said Grimy, but I interrupted him.

"The woman? You mean the boy's mother? Some might say she was the marshal's girlfriend. . . . Well, she might be the only one who didn't think so. You see, gentlemen," I saw the marshal's smile slump like melting snow off a cedar branch and I kept my eyes locked on his. "The marshal here killed her, too. Oh yes, I know it's my word against his. But bear in mind that given the number of days ago the boy was attacked matches with, by your own admittance, the date you two robbed me, we've already proved I didn't kill the boy. And then keep in mind that I was in jail last night and the marshal had the only key — he never trusted Finchy, his employee, with it, you see."

"Fascinating story, killer man." The marshal raised the rifle a few inches and shook his head as if to say, 'Too late.'

"Then how'd you get outta the jail cell?" said Grimy. I did not look away from the marshal and though we were ten feet apart and it was growing darker by the minute, I no longer saw a trace of a smile on his face, just a stare cold as stone that looked a good ten years older than a minute before. I could hear the gears grinding in his head. How did I know the woman was dead? A guess?

No, he would think, too difficult for a guess. He reached up with his free hand and lightly touched the scratches on his cheek and lips. Now he was thinking that it didn't matter. He would kill me soon and be done with it all.

"I was let out of that cell," I continued, "by none other than the killer, the one who had just come from murdering a grieving woman, widow of a murdered man, mother of a murdered child. Yessir, a real family killer. Let's see, there was Big Burl, his son, his wife. The fellow who let me out of that cell and gave me this horse — I'm probably the only man here who hasn't stolen a horse — that man was nervous, jumpy, oh, and he had three deep scratches on his face, welts on his lips. Something a person might do to another in desperation."

To the left of my field of vision I saw Grimy lean forward toward the marshal. I imagine he was looking at the lawman's face real hard, trying to pick out those scratches. The marshal flinched and one eye twitched. I smiled, something I figured a man with nothing left to lose can afford to do, and decided I'd had enough of the cute chatter.

For good or ill my natural inclination is to make things happen instead of waiting for them to happen. Not taking my eyes from the marshal, I said, "You fellas know what he told me? On the trail here, not an hour ago, this fine figure of a lawman said he's going to kill me . . . and both of you. I expect he's going to do it, too. And right about . . . now!"

I watched the marshal's forearm flex, and his hand whipped back. I dove off the far side of the bay, hoping that the quiet brother was as smart and as trustworthy as I sensed he was. I dropped low and dove for the mass of rocks to my left. I wasn't shot en route so I assumed the mute brother was less interested in killing me than his brother, Grimy, was. Or the quiet one had been shot first. Either way I made out.

As I scrambled over the looming masses of rock I heard three initial shots, the first two almost on top of each other, then a volley of perhaps a half-dozen more, and all the while were the jarring sounds of horses neighing in alarm. Then hooves thundered in two directions, some of which headed southward. The fact that I didn't have a weapon and that I knew the three men firing at each other were all criminals helped me swallow the notion that I ran from a fight, something I took no pleasure in.

I kept low, peering over the rim of rounded boulders. The light was nearly gone but I believe I counted three horses fleeing. If any were ridden, I could not tell. Three more gunshots sounded and as the last one faded I heard the high-pitched yelps of a wounded man. It wasn't the marshal and it couldn't be the mute, so Grimy had been hit. And judging from his gargled, wet screams I'd say he was gut-shot. I'd heard as much a few times in the past and it was never easy to take, even if the man was a dirty thief. I listened, the silence felt eternal.

"Dez! Dez, where are you?" It was the shot man. I heard no other sounds. I swallowed and wiped my palms on my thighs. That murdering marshal could be anywhere.

I couldn't listen to him any longer without trying to help him. If the marshal was playing possum I was done for, but fool that I was I thought I could help a dying man. Now there's a part of me I will never understand. How could I think that helping a dying man was more important than saving my own skin?

Other than Grimy's moans, the little clearing was silent. Even the soft, high breezes of a spring evening refused to rustle the new Aspen leaves. I made it to his side and he stopped moaning long enough to hiss, "Dez, I knew you'd come back. Did you . . . did you get him?"

"I'm not Dez," I said, crouching low and looking around us. "I'm the guy you bushwhacked." He stiffened and I could just make out his eyes as they widened. I patted his shoulder and said, "Don't worry, I don't carry grudges."

He seemed to buy this because he resumed his moaning. "Oh, it hurts so bad, oh god."

"Look, is your brother hit?"

Hi speech was halting, like he was trying to talk and swallow at the same time. "I . . . I don't think so. He lit out after that damn marshal. He'll get him. Dez is a good shot. Better'n me. I never was much good with a gun."

I only half heard him. Maybe Dez had chased the marshal back toward town. A horse snorted in the brush to the east, out of the clearing. "Who's there?" I said in a loud voice. "We're armed and not in any mood to continue this thing."

"Give me your gun," I whispered to Grimy. Up close, his usual filth, mingled with fear and sweat, rendered him the worst-smelling living human I have ever been near.

"I don't have it. I . . . I must of dropped it." He was panting hard now. I reached for

122

his holster but it was empty. He only carried the one gun. He moaned when I patted his waist for anything else I might use as a weapon, but no luck, no knife, nothing.

I scampered off to the right, keeping low. I had to find that pistol. It couldn't have gone far.

"Don't leave me, mister."

"Keep your voice down. I'm trying to save our hides."

He coughed and it sounded like wet gravel. I crawled around for a long time on my hands and knees, trying not to make noise. I worked my way the few feet to where I thought Grimy may have fallen, tried to picture how his gun hand might have jerked upward and dropped the pistol when he was hit. Nothing. And then a horse snorted not five feet ahead of me, beyond the bushes.

I froze, my heart seized in mid-beat, my sweating back slicked over with ice and the hair on my head turned pure white, I was sure of it. I waited a few seconds more, then reason hit me. Why would a stalking man sit a snorting horse and not do anything about it? Not moving, not creaking in the saddle. If I heard three horses run off, then this must be the fourth.

I stood half upright and felt my way into

the bushes. The horse nickered and shook its head, trying to back away. It was tangled in a thicket. And it was the bay.

"Easy boy, easy." I stroked his face and neck while I worked the reins free. He walked behind me into the clearing and his footsteps sounded normal.

The other horse, Grimy's, would be long gone by now. And with it a canteen and anything edible in the saddlebags. I was at a loss. I couldn't move Grimy in his condition, which I could hear in his coughing and wet voice. He would have to stay while I somehow wrangled help for him from town.

"I found a horse." I kneeled down on his other side, my face inches from his. "Would you like my shirt as a pillow, kid?"

"No! Don't touch me. Please leave me be. I can't take a movin'."

"Right, but I'm going to have to leave you while I head into town for help. Best just try to relax, okay kid?"

He nodded and swallowed hard and slow. Then he coughed again, and in a quiet, panting voice said, "Mister."

"Yeah?"

"For what it's worth, I believed you. About the lady and the kid and all."

"Thanks." Let's hope your brother does, I thought. "I'll be back as soon as I can."

"Mister?"

I stopped again. Time was precious now but in truth, I would listen to him all night if need be. "Yeah, kid?"

"You sure gave that bear hell. I seen it. You sure did."

"Thanks, kid. Glad I gave you something to see. Now rest easy. I'll be back with your brother. I promise." I touched his shoulder a last time. "It'll all work out fine, kid," and mounted the bay. The lie burned like a hot coal in my throat.

I heard him say, "Thanks," as we rode out of the clearing.

The night was coming off half-mooned and the trees were thick on the big slope south. I had gone a few hundred yards as fast as I dared in what I hoped was the direction of town when I heard a gunshot behind me. I reined up and listened. No second shot.

He'd held out on me. I was looking for his pistol and it must have been under him the entire time. Well, kid, I thought. You were good with a gun when it counted most.

I hesitated there for a few seconds, toying with the idea of going back for the pistol. But I knew he'd eaten the end of it and all of a sudden it didn't seem that important. I kicked hard at the bay's belly and headed toward Tall Pine, a town brimming with guns.

CHAPTER ELEVEN

In the mountains, buckskin is more durable than wool. Though not as warm, it's a decent compromise between warmth and durability. But a buckskin shirt flayed open by an enraged bear tends to let in more chill night air than I prefer, and on a crisp evening in May, the Rockies is not a warm and welcoming place. It is a place in which to be hunkered by a snapping fire, leaning in close, rereading by flame of Odysseus' tribulations in trying to find his way home.

I have always thought of myself as his opposite. I am trying to find my way away from anything resembling a home. And so I would have to conclude that the trail is my home. But there was no fire's warmth for me on that night. I was bone-tired and knew if I stood a chance of making any difference at all in my fate or the fates of others by facing down that marshal, then I would have to close my eyes, if only for a little while.

I was within ten yards of breaking from the firs and aspen when I slowed and let the bay rest. It had been a treacherous slope, steep at times, and we both needed a breather. Beyond the trees and out into the open I saw the scattered points of light of Tall Pine spread far below. Through low tree limbs and new fluttering leaves, the oil-lamp lights looked like candle flames. I wished briefly that I might be in one of those little warm homes, even in that town, just for a night.

I tied the bay's reins about a sapling. He was in no more mood than I to bolt for freedom. We'd both been through far too much in the last day. He stood still, canting a rear leg and lowering his head. I leaned down, my knees and back creaking and popping from stiffness. With a grunt and a sigh I sat at the base of a big, old pine. If I still had my hat, I would have tilted it forward over my eyes. I didn't and it didn't matter. I intended to let a few hours pass by. I wanted the town good and quiet. I figured that the wee hours would be the best time to spring a plan that doesn't exist on a town that knows you're coming. And in no time at all I was dead to the world — until the bay's throaty chuckle drew me from sleep.

I would like to say that I snapped awake,

but in truth I only staggered to my feet, gripping the rough bark of the pine and shaking my head to clear the wool someone had stuffed in there while I slept. I had no idea how long I was out, but the night had completely darkened and damp cold sneaked up into me from the ground, settled in the air, and when I looked out across the plain, low fog thick as winter quilts hovered waist high. Beyond it the town's lights had diminished to but a few, unless fog blocked the others from my view. The sweet tang of pine mixed with crisp night air and in an effort to clear my head, I drank it in.

Across this sloping plain from the direction of town, I heard hoofbeats in a steady gallop. I walked to the tree line, squinted into the dark, and drew back. They were closer than I realized — not fifty yards off. The bay stepped and nickered, fidgeting in place. I patted his neck and leaned low. I had no time to move out of the way. I rubbed my head hard with both hands, managing only to reawaken the dull throbbing of my bruised and scabbed face. The rider was coming in fast. I gambled, something I knew a little about, though not enough to wager my life. But a man's got to go all or nothing at some point in the game or settle up and slink off home. And as I said, I had no home. Time to up the ante.

"Hold it right there!" I yelled in a growl that I hoped sounded menacing. Close enough for me to make out the rider's silhouette, broad in the shoulders and with a wide, tall hat, the horse wheeled broadside to me and the man disappeared, slipping off the far side of the saddle. I heard a hammer click and then a flash that illumined the saddle and horse, the top of the wide hat. The shot sliced too high through branches and leaves. He had no idea where I was located. Then I saw the stock of a rifle rising from its boot. Good news, he outgunned me by a long shot, which is what it would be if I decided to get by him. No choice but to play the hand. I continued my bluff.

"Don't do it, mister. You're covered. Best leave the long gun in the boot and holster that hog leg." To my surprise the rifle slid back into its sheath. I doubted the pistol did the same. The horse danced a bit, but whoever it was steadied the beast. This was getting me nowhere fast. I wanted to get to that town sometime that night, and preferably in one piece. I had a hunch it wasn't the marshal. There was that hat. I'd only seen a brim that wide on one man recently. I decided to play that hunch.

"If you are who I think you are, then you'll

130

want to know about your brother. Come on out. Lead your horse and I'll do the same. But not if you have that gun in your hand."

I waited for what seemed an eternity. And I let him make the first move. It's not that I am an unfair man, but that he had an unfair advantage — at least two weapons to my none. Unless you count my ability to get into trouble. He came around the front of the horse slowly, sideways to me so as to present the least possible target. His hands, one holding the reins, were raised to chest height.

He slowed when he realized he was the first to reveal himself. I followed suit and we advanced on each other. We were fifteen feet apart before I was dead-certain it was the mute brother, and my mouth has never been drier. I figured he recognized me as well. I wouldn't say it was exactly relief that I felt, but then neither would he. We drew within five feet of each other. I nodded, said, "Dez."

He stared. Then we both stared a few seconds more, unsure of what the other might do. Finally he pointed north, upslope, back the way I had come, then shook a hand at me, palm up, urging information from me. His face seemed part of a different body. The chiseled features scowled. It was too dark to tell what was in his eyes, but I guessed I would have seen buried there behind that cold gaze a look of concern, of hope.

How to tell this man his brother had died? And how much to tell him? Would he blame me for any part of it? I was in no position to risk any more than I had to. "Your brother was shot. Pretty bad. In the gut. I tried to help him." Words were useless. The miserly moonlight broke through and let me watch that hope drain from his eyes, replaced instead with a new sadness that would never leave them for the rest of his days.

"I'm sorry," I said, but they were mere words.

He looked down at nothing, at the darkness. I was suddenly glad I hadn't taken his brother's revolver after all. If he were to find his brother's body as it was but without a gun, the man with that weapon would be in a position of having to explain himself pretty hard and fast. There would be time to worry about all that later.

"The marshal?" I said. "Did you kill him?"

He flinched as if I had awakened him, then shook his head. No such luck, I thought. He brought up a hand and slapped his left arm below the shoulder. "Did you wing him?" He nodded. A ripped-up arm is better than no hit at all.

"I need to get to that town to clear my name. Or die trying. And it wouldn't hurt my feelings a bit if I had some help doing it." He nodded, his jaw muscles clenched, and turned to mount up. "Whoa, whoa," I said, grabbing him by the same upper arm he had just slapped. He paused and stared at me, his eyes fixed hard and looking right at mine. "I can't have the marshal shot until I get him to confess somehow. And I don't have a plan as to how to do that yet. You're a witness, that's a start."

He shook his head and jerked a thumb at his parted mouth.

"I understand that you can't speak. But we'll cross that bridge when we come to it," I said, wishing he could tell me how close to town he'd been, what he'd seen. "After I get what I need from the marshal, you can have him. Does that sound like something we can agree on?"

I wanted to tell him that he owed me that much, but that feeling was in the air. Had been since he and his brother first robbed me. Thankfully, this was the brother with the conscience. Conscience enough to feel badly about what they'd done to me and conscience enough to want revenge for his brother's killing, no matter the fact that his brother was not the most likable sort. He was near enough to me that I saw the unchanging face nod twice in curt confirmation.

We mounted up and loped side by side across the plain, quiet for the first couple of minutes. Finally, I broke the silence. It dawned on me that I would be the most likely one of us to instigate a conversation. "I see now why you wear such a tall hat," I said, nodding at the neat little hole halfway up the crown of his felt.

He tipped off the hat and looked at it, poked a finger through the front hole, then its twin to the rear. He scowled again at me and plopped it back on his head and snugged it down tight.

I got the feeling that even if his brother hadn't been killed he wouldn't be a smiler. Again we rode on without me saying anything for a few minutes. I was on his right side and I gestured toward the rifle in the boot. "I'm weaponless. You mind sharing?"

He glanced at me and shook his head. He read the look of irritation on my face and explained, with gestures toward the bobbing rifle stock, that it was empty.

"No spare shells?" I asked.

He shook his head no. And he wore but

one pistol on his belt. We rode a few more paces in silence, then I said, "My things? My guns and my horse? Where are they now?"

Those jaw muscles worked hard again and he looked straight ahead. Finally, he looked at me and pointed toward the lights to which we were drawing near. We rode in silence for a few minutes more, then he placed his open hand against his chest and tilted his head to one side, looking at me. I took that as an apology, though his features still looked as if he smelled something rank. Maybe he was telling me I could stand some hot water and soap.

"Okay," I said. "I'll find them. With your help."

He nodded. Our somber mood was somewhat lifted by this exchange, but not enough. That wouldn't happen until we were through in town, come what may. We rode in silence again for a few paces, then my stomach offered a hellacious sound and he looked over at me.

"You don't happen to have any food with you? Jerky? Anything?"

The quiet man stared at me with his scowling face, then shook his head and looked forward again.

"Thanks." I was tempted to say that I was

not trying to steal from him, but I dropped it. I tried to come up with some sort of plan but other than finding a gun and then finding the marshal, hopefully in that order, the only thing I could keep my mind on was my need for food. And sleep. And water. In any order. Despite my cat nap, or maybe because of it, I felt more tired than before and the few little lights of Tall Pine that were still burning at this hour kept getting closer.

Chapter Twelve

We approached town from the northeast, cutting a wide arc in the new, fresh grass. I regretted having to leave the relative safety of the trees, but I was grateful for the fog and the increasing cloud cover that provided choppy respite from the half-moon's light. It was midnight to one o'clock in the morning, dead of the night, and we had ample time before us to do what needed to be done.

We rode for a time in a pocket in the rolling countryside and stopped at the bottom to drink from a little stream wending through. All that water on its way someplace else. I sometimes felt like water — constantly traveling, never getting anywhere in particular, and knowing I never will. I didn't instigate any more conversation, and he didn't offer any gestures my way. The water went a long way toward restoring my sapped strength.

After a few minutes we gained the far side of the long trough. Up the other side it took us less time than I expected to see the dim lights of Tall Pine, glowing dull and small at the base of the hills. It occurred to me then that any pines the town may have been named for were at best a few miles to the north, up where I had napped in the trees.

Odd how things get named. A town with no trees named after an extraordinary tree and no one thinks anything of it. An innocent man labeled a killer and no one thinks anything of it. This town was packed full of people who thought me a double-murderer, a clubber of old men, and a horse thief. I hoped I could get them to change their mind. I dug in my heels and guided the horse toward town. My companion, the mute man whose full name I did not know, rode stone-faced beside me the entire journey of perhaps three-quarters of an hour, never once looking at me unless I asked a question of him, and these I limited to what I thought he could answer with hand gestures.

The disadvantage of such a still night is that sound tends to drift over long distances. When we were still a quarter-mile from the eastern end of the main street, I slowed the bay and my companion did the same with

138

his horse.

In a low voice I asked, "When you were here did you notice how many men he has and where they are positioned?"

He shrugged, shook his head, and kept riding. I was beginning to doubt his usefulness to my mission. From what I could recall of my brief moments of exposure to the town's layout, other than its two ends, there were numerous openings onto the main street, all between buildings. Other than six or eight smaller shacks set in no pattern behind the south side of the main street, there were no other structures that made up Tall Pine. It was probably home to between sixty and seventy-five people, half of whom were probably men, and if we had to face even *half* that number, that left still more than a dozen men. The odds did not look favorable.

He stopped and pointed to his chest with that thick thumb, then pointed to the east end of the main street, jerked the thumb at me, and wagged it toward the backs of the buildings to our right, behind the north side of town.

"Split up?" I said, leaning toward him and whispering. He nodded and started forward.

"Wait a minute," I said. "We don't even know what we're doing yet."

He looked at me as if to say that it was already quite obvious to him. "Okay, go," I said. "But I need the marshal alive. Like we agreed."

He stared at me hard, then looked past me into the clouded night sky toward the hills from which we had just ridden, toward the last place and time he had seen his brother alive. Then he looked back at me and there was no mistaking the look in those eyes. He was a grieving and angry man. He was telling me that all bets were off and that I'd better reach the marshal first. He nodded once and then as one, horse and rider disappeared in a swirl of fog.

I dismounted a good fifty yards or so from the backs of the buildings and let the bay loose to graze in the sparse meadow. No need to ride on in and tie him to a rail on Main Street. He was a rare, fine horse and I couldn't help but think that the marshal made a mistake in putting me on him. I rubbed his neck and whispered, "Thanks, chum," and keeping low, I made my way toward those dark shapes.

I felt more exposed and vulnerable now than I had been on the horse. At least on horseback I had a chance at flight. On foot and with not even so much as a knife for protection, I was well and truly desperate. There were no lights in any of these buildings. And while the fog made my going slow, I was relieved to know that it would also make spotting me a difficult task. I slipped into a gap between two darkened buildings and paused there. Just enough room for my shoulders. Why did they build them so close and how did they manage to swing hammers when they finally decided on such a spot? My mystification at mankind sometimes knows no bounds.

I wished I had my hat to pull down over my face. I was used to drawing attention at the best of times, that is to say when my face hasn't been used as a snack by a grizzly, but my still-swollen head and cut ear would draw attention faster than a sign around my neck that read, "Killer returns." I stuck to the shadows. It was easy. Despite the reception I expected from the marshal, the town appeared to be asleep.

My boot toes knocked against something that felt like firewood and I stopped dead. I'd wager it was only loud to me, but it was enough to keep my heart from beating for a half-minute or so. Pretty soon up ahead of me I heard a pair of boots stepping slow, the heels echoing off the wooden walkway. I paused, waited for the sound to recede, and

I made my way to the mouth of the alley. I kept low and since the clouds had slipped away from the moon for the moment, I stayed well in the shadows.

I was between two shops, I think, looking for the saloon, and guessed it to be three more buildings down toward the east. As I turned to retreat back down the alley I heard a tearing sound across the street. I froze. A match flared and the glow framed a hat tipped forward. Someone lighting a smoke. Could be a person who doesn't sleep well. Could be someone waiting for a killer to return to town. Could be one of many such people. I backed up and squeezed between the two buildings.

The back door to the saloon was unlocked. I opened it enough to slip inside and felt my way along a wall. From the piled empty crates and rags I guessed I was in a store room. And not two feet away, in the dark, I heard the unmistakable sound of a man snoring. A drunk sleeping it off. Not for the last time that night did I wonder what I was doing. That bay was a good horse and could have carried me far away by morning.

I held my breath and deliberated. In too deep now, I thought. And I stepped toward where I hoped the door to the saloon might be. I reached out a hand and touched a wooden slide latch.

In no time, I was behind the bar and feeling with the flat of my hands everything but what I wanted. I nearly gave up when my fingertips brushed the cold, rounded steel of a gun barrel. I traced it down and it was the same double-barrel shotgun that fat Slim had used to knock some sense out of me. My crabbing fingers were doubly rewarded with three shells next to it on the shelf. I pocketed one, cracked open the gun — sure enough it wasn't loaded. I slid two shells home, clicked the gun closed, and straightened my back.

There is nothing so different from its daytime self as a saloon at night. Whatever else he might be, from what I could see Slim at least tried to keep the place tidy. Chairs were upended on tabletops, a sure sign that the floor was swept, but the dead smells of stale beer and smoke, when not being added to, flowered in the dark. I imagined this room a few hours before, full of men wearing guns and swearing oaths to haul that killer up the nearest tree.

As I turned back to the store room I saw the pickled eggs jar on the back of the bar. I didn't even hesitate. The wood bung lifted with no noise but I made a fair amount of sound as I plunged my hand in and crammed an egg whole into my mouth. I was on my second when I remembered the sleeping man in the other room. I tried to keep my grunting and slurping to a minimum. I reached in and my hand splashed in a couple of inches of vinegar and nothing else. All the eggs were gone. I cursed the fat bartender for a lazy man, and set the bung back on the jar.

Inside the store room I heard the steady, heavy breathing of a man in the full throes of deep sleep. I envied him. Then my toes nudged a bottle. It clinked against another and I reached down to steady them and succeeded in knocking them over. Never have I heard a sound as loud. Thousands of bottles must have toppled into each other before they stopped rolling and clanking.

The sleeping man was now awake and saying, "Uh? Uh?" I backed toward the bar, but I had already closed the store-room door behind myself. Too tidy, that's me. I crouched low, the shotgun held in front of me. What little moonglow there was from the open outside door was blocked out as a massive mountain of a man rose from the shadows.

"Who's there?" said a deep voice, not sounding drunk in the least.

I hesitated, then said, "That you, Slim?"

"Yeah? Who's there?"

I aimed for the top of the mountain, and as I felt the gun butt meet resistance, I said, "I owed you one."

The mountain crumbled in a loud mess of bottles and crates and many other unseen items that also made a heck of a lot of noise. I tripped over more bottles and added to the din. Once outside I didn't hear any more sounds, and figured Slim really would be asleep for a while now — and would wake up with something not unlike a hangover. Served him right.

Unfortunately, all that noise alerted not a few folks around town. The mumbles and sharp yells of voices reached me as I dashed down the row of hulking structures that appeared from the murky gloom only as I came upon them in the dark. It seemed that the windows of every building I ran behind lit up almost too soon as I passed, the warm glow of oil lamps casting squares of light on the otherwise black ground below, fog swirling through the patterns of light. It was almost as if the entire town had been waiting for a signal of some sort. Had I given it to them?

Two gunshots from opposite ends of town cracked the night. I angled away from the buildings and into the murky night, all the while headed for the end of the street and the marshal's office. And then a rapid volley of gunshots and the jarring sound of a horse thundering up the hard-packed dirt of the street seemed to awaken the rest of the town. I saw a blur of horse and rider in lampglow between two well-spaced buildings.

"He's over there," someone shouted. "Headed up the street. Get him!"

"It's the killer. Look out, he's got a gun! Look out!"

I heard women scream, men shout, and children whimper. They thought it was me. But I knew it was Dez, the mute thief. And he hadn't made a ruckus until I raised the dead with my display of bottle tipping in the saloon store room. It occurred to me that he was drawing attention from me to himself by providing one heck of a distraction — like a dove landing in a box of hungry cats. He was helping me, but he might get himself killed in the process. I wondered if he really cared. Perhaps that had been his plan all along.

Lights erupted in nearly every building, and there were others — lanterns swinging in tight arcs as they were carried across the foggy street. The gunshots kept on and I had to admire the mute's sand, his ploy worked. I saw more than a dozen people head toward the far end of the street following the shooting horseman. Then I heard a rifle crack and no other guns after that.

As I ran across the street I was relieved to find this end of town seemed deserted and still somewhat dark. Dead ahead of me the marshal's office windows offered a flickering orange light. Good. Someone was home. I only hoped it was the marshal. What was I going to do with him? I didn't know. Hold him prisoner and stave off the entire town until he confessed? Would he? Probably not. Could I force it out of him? Maybe, but I'd need a witness to verify the confession. Would the town believe me? And could I hold the town off long enough? That all depended on how much they liked him. From what I'd seen, to call him popular would be understating his standing among these people.

Loyalty's a strange thing. A town will rally around even its least-liked member if only because he's one of them. And no one here would dare go against the grain — Tall Pine would be a dangerous place indeed for anyone slighting its beloved members.

As I left the street I ran through the light cast by the marshal's office lamp. It was for a moment, but as I passed through it, I heard someone shout, "I seen 'im!" Great. As I headed by the marshal's office, I peeked in the side window. It was small enough for me to see that unless he was hiding in the hallway or one of the two cells, he wasn't there. Probably following in the wake of the mute's ruckus.

I jumped into the dark, narrow alley between the marshal's office and a little warehouse with the cramped livery out back. It was the same spot where the marshal had the bay waiting for me the night before. I passed through the soft smells of dusty hay and old manure.

I hugged the backs of the buildings on the south side and made my way down the street one building at a time. Despite the shotgun's substantial heft — it was like running with a log — I was more than pleased that I was armed. Once the three shells were spent, I could upend the gun and use it as one heck of a club. I would go down swinging. Don't count yourself out of the race just yet, Roamer, I told myself.

I was now behind what I took to be the back garden off the tallest structure in town, the general mercantile, which means I was more than halfway down the street. I crouched low and looked back. Nobody tracking me, that I could see. The pungent smell of fresh horse manure wafted around me. I'd probably stepped in it. Wouldn't be the first, hopefully not the last. At that minute, I could have been rolled in it and it wouldn't matter. I was alive and had a chance, thin as it was, of making things right. The mute had at least bought me that. I wasn't about to waste that gift. I hoped he'd hightailed it out of town and re-grouped. I was sure I'd need his help in the near future.

This was as good a place as any to wait for the hubbub to die down. I expected that after a short while the marshal would gain back his confidence and return to the jail. I leaned against a rough plank wall and worked on gaining an edge on my heavy breathing. Voices at the far end of the street grew louder. I stood up, still careful to stay against the wall.

The voices increased in strength, but they weren't coming closer. It was a crowd's noise, roaring and primitive in its collective urgency. There were no intelligible sounds at this distance, but several voices rose above the rest in louder, more urgent shouts. And then one of the voices growled, "Kill him!" and I knew they had captured the mute.

CHAPTER THIRTEEN

I managed to creep forward one step at a time, keeping low and grasping the shotgun in front of me, inches from a swing-and-shoot position. The grumbles and shouts grew louder. The closer I drew to the crowd, the more distinctly I heard the words being spoken. The dominant voice was familiar to me. Of course it was the marshal, and aside from the occasional outburst from the jostling crowd, his words held sway over all others. I stopped midway up the last alley, leaned against a wall, and listened.

"This here's one of the killers, all right. I was ambushed today in the hills, looking for the ringleader of this plague of murderers and thieves that was brought down on our little town. A plague we don't deserve but one that we will have to deal with ourselves. It's up to us to protect the lives of our children against these animals."

The crowd barked its support, arms raised

in the air. By this time I had made my way up the last alley on the street and the outer edges of the crowd pulsed not fifteen feet away, their half-dressed assemblage lit by lanterns and oil lamps held aloft in shaking fists. I crept forward and peeked around the corner of the building. The roughness of the vertical planking felt cool against my cheek.

"Now folks, now folks. You know I've suffered not a little bit these past few days. Arietta, the love of my life, and her dear boy — James was like a son to me. . . ." He paused here and the crowd grew quiet. A woman whose hair hung like wet yarn put her hand to her mouth and shook her head. Men's voices murmured, heads nodded, jaw muscles were set tight, and a few women whimpered. I heard the marshal's voice crack, heard a snuffling sound, then he continued. "I'm sorry, folks. It's a rough time, it truly is. But we have to be strong. We cannot let this scourge devour us, all right?"

I had to admit the marshal was a pretty good orator, if a touch melodramatic. What would he do with the Bard, I wonder? I risked peeking my head out further but still could only make out more of the crowd. The marshal was too far to my left and hidden from my view.

"I was shot today, but the doctor says I'll be fine."

Shouts of sympathy and encouragement greeted this announcement.

"But it was this man, this evildoer, who got me. I shot his companion in the woods, but there still roams the one we know for a fact who killed dear young James and his mother, my beloved. That killer is also the one who broke out of jail and clubbed Finchy in the head. And then had the audacity to steal a horse! These crimes cannot stand." His voice rose in a high, passionate plea. Again, the crowd's mingled sounds surged in the chill air.

"The only way to show killers that we are not afraid of their evil is to make an example of those we catch in the act. This murdering thief took advantage of our hospitality and played on our emotions, and now he must be made an example of. What should we do with one who rides with a child murderer? With one who robs and murders innocent people instead of doing an honest day's work? I leave it up to you, my fellow citizens."

The crowd roared and pressed in close to its center, arms and heads shook with rage, legs lashed out, kicking at each other and at the unfortunate man in their midst. From my position in the shadows at the head of the alley I saw through the legs of the jostling figures, and already the mute was stretched out on the ground, perhaps had been the entire time the marshal made his speech.

That final rifle shot I had heard must have felled him from his mount, of which I now saw no sign. I was surprised to see that without his tall hat the mute had a head full of thick, dark hair. It was still nighttime, yes, but his dark hair gave him a more youthful appearance, putting him closer in age to his brother than I had originally suspected.

His body twitched and rose and flopped with each striking boot. Until some in the crowd resorted to pistols he tried to defend himself, pulling a leg up, covering his face with an arm. But then each pistol shot jerked the dark man's gaunt frame into a prone stillness.

Within seconds it was plain that Dez was dead. I wished that the rifle shot that had wrenched him from the back of his horse had killed him instantly, but it did not. The agonies he must have suffered in silence tightened me inside. Not that his pain mattered to the frantic, clawing townspeople.

In all my years roaming the lands west of

the Mississippi River, I have witnessed such savage collective attacks, though mostly in the wild — wolves will attack their own for various practical reasons, as will coyotes, bears, and wild cats. Certain species of birds will do the same, and I have read that there are many creatures in foreign lands that behave thusly, though never without sufficient reason.

But was blind rage reason enough to kill a man? Some would say yes. I had my doubts. I have been in the midst of foul war, but never seen such a savage attack among humans as I witnessed that night. The long shadows of the flickering lamps pulled at their leering faces. I saw bulging eyes and flying spittle adding to the general unkempt appearance of people awakened in a night already filled with tension when they lay down a few short hours before.

The frenzy slowed, the dead man's clothes were now a dark smear of blood and dirt. He flopped as if he were nothing more than sacks of loose jellies squeezed into a man's shape. His hands were mangled stumps, and one of the men whose face I recognized from that rainy day in the same street a few days before grasped the mute by his thick, dark hair and jerked his head upward. He looked closely at the man's face and said,

"He ain't got no tongue! No wonder he never so much as whimpered!"

This news should not have shocked me, but nonetheless it felt like a dunking in a cold stream. And judging from the hands raised to faces and the steps taken backward, it affected others in the same way. Another man, burly and short with a red beard and no hair on his head said, "Yeah, but what'd he do to get hisself cut like that? Can't have been good." The crowd responded with nods of assent and closed in to see the sight for themselves.

I heard myself moan. I felt chilled, as if a fever had gripped me. I had been too late to help him. And preventing them from desecrating his body would have resulted in nothing but my own grisly death at the hands of this savage mob. I backed from the main street and crouched my way down the length of the short alley.

I looked left, then right, and emerged from the back end of the alley. The jail would be the place to await the marshal. It would have plenty of weapons and coffee simmering on the woodstove too, which I sorely needed. I retraced my steps behind the short row of shops until I came to the dusty little livery with its oddly comforting smells of animals at rest.

And to my left in the musty darkness I heard a hammer click back into that worst position of all. I turned my head slowly. A match scratched and bloomed, a lamp glowed, and the marshal's face, grinning and sweating, despite the coolness of the hour, quavered into view. "Well, all right. Welcome back to Tall Pine, killer man. I trust you enjoyed the festivities."

He leaned against a beam. Even in that low, murky light I could see he was changed. His face was sweaty and pale and seemed to have shrunk in on itself since a few hours before when I last saw him in the woods. But the effects of the bullet wound in his shoulder didn't change what I saw him as — a vicious, manipulative murderer.

"That wasn't necessary," I said, jerking my head back behind me in the direction of the murder. "That man was innocent." The voices of the crowd picked up again.

"Innocent. . . ." His smile faded and he said the word as if it reminded him of something long forgotten. "Are any of us all that innocent, killer man?"

He backed into the little stable, holding his pistol steady on me. Hay was more strewn than stacked, and full sacks of feed leaned in piles. "Come on in," he said. "Oh, and rest that scattergun by the door, will ya?"

I did as he said and for a split second I thought of bolting into the night, but I felt sure he had someone waiting in the shadows behind me. I wouldn't get far. I stepped into the stable. He waved me around to where he was standing and he backed himself toward the door.

I figured that I had reached my end. So now that I faced the cause of this mess, I wasted no time. "What did you do to her, marshal?"

He answered my question with one of his own. "What did you tell her, drifter? Way I figure it, you said something to make her think I killed her damned bawling brat boy. She come at me swingin' a knife. Wasn't nothing could be done but defend myself."

I asked my question again, quieter this time. "What did you do to her?"

He kept the pistol pointed right at my chest, sighed, and wagged his jaw back and forth, thinking, weighing his response. Finally, in a voice as low as my own, he said, "Same thing I done to the boy. Just pinched it off right there." He tweezered his Adam's apple with his thumb and forefinger. "Ain't no more blathering that way, all right."

He was still smiling, even after admitting murder to me.

"Why? What did they ever do to you?"

"Funny," he said. "That's what she asked me. I told her they ain't done nothing yet, but they would. Give 'em enough time, they always do."

"That bruise on her cheek," I said, trying to keep him talking. The more I knew, even if no one else heard, the more I might be able to use later to convince someone I was innocent. If later ever came. And the more distracted I kept him, the more chance I had of outmaneuvering him. I didn't really believe it, but it felt better than to admit to myself I was already a dead man.

"Oh, that wasn't nothing," he said, his subject matter bringing that damnable smile to his face. "She struggled a little at first. That's what you do with a woman like that. Take the starch out, then you got something you can use. Otherwise she's always trying to get the better of you."

I wanted to beat him to pieces right there. I'm not a small man and I don't use my fists all that often, but I wanted to attack him like I had never wanted to beat a man before. It was his revolver that kept me still.

"And then?" I asked, my jaw set so tight I could barely squeeze the words between my teeth.

"For a walking dead man, you are a curious sort of fella." He worked his mouth again, as if chewing on something. I'd seen him do this before, in the saloon, and I knew he was weighing what to tell me. The prideful man in him won out. He leaned forward, his pale, sweating face waxen in the flickering lamp light. "I give it to her." He smiled at the memory. "Was a long time comin' and I finally give it to her. Right where you are now, matter of fact. On them grain sacks."

I glanced down as if the scene was still visible. I could only imagine the terror she felt.

"And the boy?" I asked. "He knew, didn't he?"

"Pretty smart for a dead man." He chewed some more then said, "Saw the whole thing, that nosey kid did. Nothing a kid should be watching. That's a man and a woman's private time. But he needed a lesson anyway. Too long without a daddy was his problem."

"What's yours?" I said.

Emotion drained from his face. He looked like a corpse. "You," he said.

I saw his hand muscles bunch as his fingers tightened on the walnut grip of the pistol. And then he fired. I had enough time to almost get shot in the chest. When I saw his hand squeeze on that six-gun I turned my body from him, duel style, and it was enough to avoid dying, but not enough to avoid getting skinned. The bullet tore across my chest, taking a little of me with it and leaving a trail that would no doubt make people in public bath houses step further away from me in future.

He had enough time to pull back his hammer again and that's when we heard the unmistakable clicks of the shotgun hammers, and Finchy stepped into view behind the marshal.

"Naw," he said. "Marshal's problem is he talks too much." He poked the marshal in the back with the business end of the shotgun and said, "Drop it away, marshal."

I watched the marshal's eyes, hoping like mad I'd get an indication before he pulled that trigger again. But he stared at me and smiled. Then he said quietly, "All right, all right," and spun around fast, dropping to his back on the floor at the same time.

The marshal counted too much on surprise and didn't count enough on an old man's lifetime of experience in dealing with adversity. Finchy sidestepped and rapped the marshal's gun arm, sending the pistol spinning into the darkness of the stable floor. A low whinny sounded from the dark behind me, deeper in the stable.

The marshal's face showed unmasked anger and he pulled the arm tight to his chest. "What in hell are you up to, Finchy? Have you lost your mind? Give me my pistol and I'll forget you did that!"

Finchy, his head swaddled high in a bandage of some sort, stuck out his bottom jaw and squinted his eyes as if considering the proposition. Finally he said, "I guess prob'ly not."

The marshal tried to stand, but Finchy pushed him back down with a boot to his thigh. "Eh eh eh, keep 'er where she is, marshal, 'til I say you can move."

"You —"

"And keep your mouth shut tight for now." He bent forward at the waist and said, "All right?"

If angry eyes were lethal weapons, Finchy would be a dead man. I peeled my buckskin apart where the bullet tore a trail and pushed the leather hard into the narrow bleeding wound to help staunch the blood flow.

"You gonna make it, big fella?"

I looked up and nodded. "Thanks to you, yes."

Finchy looked back down at the marshal but said to me, "Well, truth be told I wasn't all that sure about you until I seen what they did to that poor soul up the street. I couldn't stop them. Too late anyway. He was shot in the back by this one here and then I seen this rascal slink off after he riled up all them fools." He still held the shotgun in both hands, aimed right at the marshal's chest. "So I followed him." He shook his head at the man and said, "And of course I heard everything he just told you." Finchy looked up at me and said, "Sorry 'bout that nick he give you. I didn't think he was that fast. Course, I should have known. He's proved me wrong before."

Finchy stretched to his full height, which barely reached to my shoulder, and said, "Enough of this jawing. We got us a crowd to deal with."

I picked up the marshal's revolver from the straw and said, "You think that's a good idea? I'm not so sure they're ready for what you may have to tell them."

"Better listen to him, Finchy. Killer man's speaking true."

Finchy squinted at the marshal. "You can stand up, but if you open your mouth again, so help me I'll rap them pearly whites with these twin barrels."

I checked the pistol's chambers, popped out a few shells from the marshal's gun belt, and topped it off.

Finchy grabbed the lantern's handle. It squeaked and he stepped back and motioned for the marshal to walk ahead of him. "Nice and slow, marshal." Then to me he said, "I still don't know exactly what's going on, but I do know he's about the worst thing ever happened to this town. And if you'd been here from the beginning, all them hard times, you'd know that's saying a lot. Now git up there." He put a boot to the marshal's backside and pushed him toward the alley.

I followed the little man, carrying the pistol and breathing deeply for the first time all day, thanking every god I'd ever heard of, Indian and white. And then I made up some for good measure. I wasn't out of the woods yet by a long shot, but Finchy's confidence went a good way toward making me feel like I stood a chance of getting out of this town alive and free of accusation.

We reached the front of the buildings and the marshal turned right toward the jailhouse. "Wrong way," said the wiry older man and he thumped the marshal hard in his wounded shoulder. The lawman took in a quick gasping breath and his legs weakened before he caught himself and straightened. The dark stain on the back of his shirt

163

grew wet with fresh blood. Finchy knew what he was doing.

CHAPTER FOURTEEN

We stepped out into the street. The crowd from the far end had moved in our direction, one man ahead of the others. Light from a dozen lamps and lanterns cast strange shadows on the faces and clothes of the mob.

"Finchy?" said the man in the lead, the white of his undershirt glowing beneath his hatless head, his suspenders flopping against his thighs. "Finchy, what's happening there? We heard a shot."

Finchy stepped forward. "Howdy, Clem. Surprised you heard anything, what with all the hootin' and shootin' you been doing."

The man he called Clem, I realized, was the one who had lifted the mute's head by the hair and first peered into his sagged mouth. Clem held up a lantern at face-height and squinted at us. "Finchy, that the marshal with you?"

'In for a penny, in for a pound,' was a

favorite saying of someone I once knew. It seemed appropriate here so I swallowed and stepped forward a couple of paces out of the shadows beside the marshal. Clem's face showed his surprise and he said, "What's going on here, Finchy? That's the killer!"

As I listened to the mounting tumult of the crowd I noticed the first signs of dawn. Soon we would not need lanterns, but for now the air around us had barely begun to shift from black to the first hint of gray. I realized then how tired I was. It had been a long time since I slept well, full of food and satisfied. The bursts of excitement that come from surprise and shock can carry a man quite a distance, but any I experienced had long since worn off and I now wanted sleep.

Someone yelled, "Kill the killer!" and I straightened and gritted my jaws tight, forcing myself to attention.

The crowd advanced on us, hooting and howling in their bloodlust, but hesitant, too. The presence of their leader coupled with someone they knew to be a friend and someone else they were convinced was a murderer instilled in them a confused caution. But they advanced, nonetheless. Finchy raised the shotgun, angling it well above their heads, and pulled a trigger. The single boom startled shrieks from a few of them, men and women alike, and as a group they stopped.

"That's far enough!" he said.

"Have you lost your senses, Finchy?" said Clem, while others shouted assent and shook fists. "That man's the killer."

"Well then, it looks to me like he'd fit in right smart with you all."

Nothing but angry shouts could meet such a claim, and that's what we got. I stepped forward and said, "Now look —" but Finchy shushed me.

"Better let me do the talking, boy," he said out of the side of his mouth. "They know me. They won't hurt me but they sure as heck won't think twice about killing you."

The marshal giggled. "Better listen to him, killer man. Finchy's highly thought of in this town, now ain't you, old man?"

With the speed of a snapped whip Finchy's gnarled old farmer's hand lashed out and caught the marshal square on the cheek, snapping the man's head to the side. The marshal held his head there and a grim look, less smile than a smug plan of revenge, was written on his glowing red face. "You better win them over, Finchy. Or there's gonna be hell to pay."

"These are my people, marshal. Not yours."

"All right, old man. We'll see."

"Clem, you come another step closer and so help me. . . ." Clem backed down and set the lantern on the ground in front of him. He wore no guns about his waist. But there were others behind him who did. I held my ground, though I knew I would make an easy target. Long shadows traveled up Clem's body and made him appear tall. He held out his arms in a calming gesture to the people behind him, then folded them across his chest.

Finchy, for the first time, looked to me as though he was nervous or unsure of himself. He licked his lips and held the shotgun two-handed before him like a shield. "You folks forget who started this town? It was me and Mother come here, let's see, how old is Slim here? He's pretty near twenty-eight, I reckon. And poor few of you know this, but he was this town's first-born citizen."

I looked behind Finchy to where he had gestured. At the edge of the shadows stood Slim, that mountain of a man, as tall and wide as ever, his massive hands on his hips, a bull stare directed at the crowd. The only change from when I'd last seen him, at least in the daylight, was that he, like his father, wore a white bandage, not unlike a turban, about his head. Slim's wrap job, however, was sloppy and not nearly as impressive in height as Finchy's.

That he was Finchy's son was quite a shock to me. How was that possible? I wondered, comparing the two men. If Finchy weighed as much as one of Slim's legs, I would be surprised. I also knew I was between a rock and another rock and it was going to take a cool bit of discussion or a further blow to his head before I might get away from Slim so easily this time.

"Mother named this town after the prettiest thing we seen when we got here," Finchy continued. "Them tall pines on the ridge up yonder, lording over this little valley like it was the most special spot on this green earth. We staked the claim to all this land in this valley, pretty near as far as a man can see on a good day. Wasn't nobody else around, so we had at it. We were making it work, too.

"Then folks started coming out this way, drifting along like, looking for a special place to live out their lives in peace. Just like Mother and me. First a single man or a young family, passing through. Then you come, Clem. You used to be in dry goods back, where was it? St. Louis? You come out here to start fresh. You stopped here and stayed a while. And we enjoyed your company. You thought you might like to try it here, so me and Mother talked it over and agreed to sell a piece to you, pretty soon we done the same for others. You two — I see you back there, Clarence and Julia.

"And then seems you all come in droves. Couldn't hardly keep a tally or a number on it. Pretty soon we give up on it altogether and figured the good Lord was providing us with friends. It wasn't no problem, long as I had my own plot of land where I set up my little farm down the road a piece. And we never asked a payment on any of that land you all have now. All them spreads outside of town. Yours, there Ruell and yours, too, Boris and Olga. Got right fine little farms now. Sure, some of you paid us, but ain't none of that lasted too long, nor could it, not when we're all so far from any place where it's easy to get supplies and such. Money come dear, and truth be told we loaned every penny of that money back to you all over again, plus some."

The few faces that were still looking up at him, at us, were wrinkled in thought. If Finchy had started out his speech nervous or concerned, he didn't show it now. Passion for his subject had warmed his speech.

"And most of you would not have made it through your first few winters and summers too, without help, be it food or money or tools. Hell, I can't remember the amount of times I've showed up here and there with my mules for spring plowing.

"And my boy, many is the time he's worked all day down to our place and then walked to your farm, Jordy, and tucked right in so's you'd get your hay in, too. And nary a thank-you among you. Well I ain't looking for such now, but I tell you one thing. You kill this man," he pointed the business end of that shotgun at me and I wanted to step backward, "like you done to that poor devil lyin' in the road yonder, and by god I tell you what," he was trembling now, hoisting that shotgun aloft like a banner and waving it like an extension of his arm. The first few rows of people in the crowd shied back as if someone was thrusting a snake at them. "It'd be like you was shooting me and my kin."

There was a lengthy pause, and that short main street was as close to dead quiet as it would ever be. Clem broke the spell. "That's crazy talk, Finchy. He's a killer!"

"It ain't crazy, 'cause he's not the killer. I'm saying you got the wrong man. The killer is this here marshal who's duped you

171

all for months now into thinking he's pretty near the representative of the Lord Almighty right here on earth."

Murmurs grew from the crowd, followed by shouts. "Oh, I was taken in, too, by all his slick talk and fancy, big town ways. But I been closer to him than most of you all, working a bit at the jail, helping to make ends meet. And I can tell you one thing. He ain't who he makes out to be. Nosiree."

"Prove it!"

"Well now I will. You all know I got a nasty knock on the head. When I come to, yes the prisoner was gone but the only person who had keys to that cell was the marshal. Ain't no other way in or out. And them keys was right on the floor beside me."

"He could have grabbed the keys off the marshal," said Clem.

Finchy nodded. "He coulda. But that ain't what the marshal told us, is it?"

The crowd mumbled something. Clem said, "Marshal told us the man surprised you and took off."

"I know what he said, but it ain't the truth. I ever lied to you, Clem? To any of you? And something else, while I'm at it, I brung over a whole heaping tray of Mother's hot chicken dinner with biscuits. And when I woke up it was all spilled from where the

172

marshal had cold conked me on the head. But ain't none of that food was missing. The entire chicken was there, all the food, all the biscuits. Why, I don't even think a lick of that gravy was touched.

"Now you tell me, would a man who hadn't eaten in days leave one of Mother's perfectly cooked chickens right there when he could have grabbed that on his way out the door to freedom? No, sir. Only a man who was forced out of the cell by the man with the keys could have been made to step right over that chicken even though all the hunger in his stomach told him to pick it up. Only a man who had a gun to his back wouldn't dare such a thing."

The crowd murmured, Clem rubbed a small, pink hand over the stubble on his jaw.

Finchy nodded, "Yeah, gravy and fresh pie, hot coffee. The works. Because the marshal here hadn't let me feed the prisoner for more than a day, never once let me feed him the whole time he was in that cramped little jail. All Mother's cooking going to waste."

A murmur crawled through the crowd.

"All you people at one time or another had Mother's cooking. You know what it'll do for you. Why look at Slim here," Finchy pointed with the shotgun at the big man behind him. No one smiled.

"Now if the marshal's so blamed great then why didn't he let this man eat?"

Truth be told all that talk of missed food set my stomach to rumbling like it had never rumbled before in my entire life. I'm sure the marshal heard it. And probably Clem and the others, too.

Clem walked forward. Right beside him was the same man in an unbuttoned striped shirt and dark pants who a short time before I had seen landing boot blows to the mute's flopping head. Finchy spun on them with the shotgun. Slim stood straighter and the marshal stiffened as I jammed the pistol into his ribs. He looked at me and I knew he was vowing to himself to kill me as soon as he was able.

Clem raised his hands. "Now Finchy, we're old friends. And you know I'd trust you with my life, but what you're saying ain't making sense. You got any proof?"

"Look, folks. I done a heap of talking here tonight. More than I care to ever again, all to once, but I got to tell you. I took a gamble on most of you all and up until tonight I never had much cause to regret my decision. Trust me this time, too. Don't let this man," he wagged a hand at the marshal, "make you any more sour inside

174

than he already has."

The marshal laughed and shook his head for a long time. Finchy half turned from the crowd and said, "What's so all-fired funny, marshal?"

"Finchy, you're a good man and I appreciate your help in the jail but you don't have any idea what's going on in this world nowadays, do you? I warned you that you better make this good. But you ain't doing it. You're on the short end now, old man."

I felt that urge to strike him rise in me again. I wanted to punch his face, but that would only serve to stir up the crowd. Once again Clem made to advance toward us.

"That's far enough, Clem," said Finchy. "Keep it there 'til I've had my say. Far as proof goes, that's what I been giving you, ain't it?"

Clem stopped and shrugged. "I haven't heard enough to convince me of anything yet, Finchy." The crowd murmured its assent. Clem, emboldened by the support of the crowd behind him, advanced one more step. I could tell that Finchy was about to falter. I had to say something.

"What about the blacksmith who died not long ago?" I said. My hoarse voice made them all spin their heads my way. "It seems mighty suspicious to me that he would die

175

just as the stranger arrives, who happens to be a lawman — or so he says. Did anybody check up on him before hiring him? Every lawman has references of some sort. Too late now, but isn't it convenient that he turns up just as the blacksmith is found dead? And then don't you all think it's mighty suspicious when that same black-smith's son and wife are found murdered? None of this happened before this man came to your quiet town."

Clem stared at me. "Two of them things happened when you came to town. How do you explain that, stranger?" He had me there. I couldn't explain it enough to convince them. And my only two true alibis were now dead. I had to think of something to say. And despite the fact that this was my last plea for reason, I felt the thread slip from my fingers. The crowd advanced as a whole, seething mass. All that talk for nothing. They were too worked up. Slim strode forward to meet them, moving his massive bulk in front of Finchy.

Clem and his chubby chum tucked into Slim's ample midsection with fervor. The people behind them, emboldened by this reckless activity, swarmed the big man and his father. I knew I was seconds away from being engulfed by the madness unfolding before me.

I backed up with the marshal, dragging him by the neck toward the fading shadows on the boardwalk, his hands clawing at my tightening arm. I jammed the pistol barrel hard against his temple. I had to get far enough away from the approaching crowd to use the marshal as a hostage, if only to free Slim and Finchy from certain death at the hands of the mob. I dragged him, kicking and grabbing, backward as fast as I could. If I stayed out in the open, one careful shot from that crowd would stop dead in its tracks any hope for a future for any of us, whether they wanted to hear it or not.

I heard Finchy cry out in pain. "My boy!" he shouted. "My baby boy! What have you done to my boy?" The crowd abruptly halted, even the few who headed my way. A woman's voice said, "Back off, give them space!"

And that's when I saw big Slim laid out flat on his back with his little father leaned over him. His hands were on either side of Slim's wide face and he cried out, "My boy! My baby boy!"

The white bandage swaddling Slim's head was now fast seeping red. The crowd grew quiet and the people who seconds before were lurching for blood now stood still in the middle of their main street, listless and deflated, their vigor drained away. They looked genuinely ashamed.

Cackling laughter cracked the silence. It came from the marshal. I jerked him but he pulled free from my grasp. I cocked the pistol but he didn't even look back at me. He slapped his leg with his good hand and laughed. I let him. It could do no harm. "Just like a cow," he said, pointing at Slim. "It don't take much to bring a big man down. Too dumb for their own good. Looked like a dropped log, same as that blacksmith. You'd think they were twins."

As if on cue, the heads of the crowd swung toward him.

"Surprised?" he said, laughing. "You shouldn't be. You're too dumb to know otherwise."

Clem shook all over as if gripped by a fever. He let out a roar of anguish, spittle flew from his mouth, and he lunged at the marshal. I stepped forward and held the revolver out straight. Clem's boot struck the bottom step and he pitched forward, his forehead jamming against the tip of the barrel. The pink skin puckered around that deadly end. He held that pose on his knees, his mouth drooling, his face puffed and red with rage. "What are you doing?" he yelled at me. His head shook. "He did this!"

"No," I said. "You did this. All of you." I looked up at the despondent crowd. "It won't be what you want to hear, but you're going to hear it. Now let the man speak." I held the gun there until Clem exhaled a stuttering breath, the sweat and blood draining from his face. He nodded and I took a step back. A perfect small circle stood out like a wart on his forehead.

"And if I don't?" said the marshal. His mouth sneered, his blond hair hung limp and matted to his forehead, and his blue eyes glittered like snake eyes in the early light. That perfect nose pointed straight at me and on his cheek, evidence of the last thing that poor woman had to endure on this earth. The scratches glowed until that's all I saw before me.

"You started this," I yelled, and swung that pistol hard at that unmarred face. The back of my hand and the back of the gun caught that vile man's perfect nose square in the middle of the long, straight bridge, the weight of the steel tool lending hard, crushing heft to the blow. I felt something snap. He screamed and staggered to the porch railing, covering his face with both hands. Thick liquid, not yet red in the growing light, poured through his fingers, ran off his chin, and pooled on the porch planking, eventually finding its way through cracks and off the edge, where it stringed down into the dirt.

"Now finish it." I said, pointing the pistol at the marshal. "And make it right. I am in no mood for games."

A collective gasp steamed forth from the crowd. That's rich, I thought, after what they did. Finchy watched me with wide eyes, and there was Slim now sitting up and leaning impossibly against his small father. My hand throbbed and I didn't care if it was broken. Nothing had felt so good or so right in a long time.

"We're all waiting," I said. He was still moaning. He turned to me, his eyes now red and watering. He swayed as if drunk and said, "All right."

He stood up straight, took his hands from his face to reveal a wrecked version of himself. His nose was a flopped smear pushed to the side of its former spot, and his top lip was split wide and ran with blood. Beneath this two teeth were missing. A few women in the front of the crowd smarted as if they themselves had been struck. He smiled, raised his hands, and beckoned the crowd to move in closer.

Again they did as he said, and again they stood still before him.

CHAPTER FIFTEEN

"I come here by accident. I'd been out Nevada way working a claim with a cousin of mine. We come to words and I left. Stopped here on my way to St. Louis. Thought I recognized a fella who'd bought a handful of claims out there in the mine fields. Large man he was and he'd got himself homesick, went back to his kin, wherever that was. We all thought he was nuts, place was played out when he bought, but right before I left some new activity kicked up. Looked promising. Only most of it was on that big fella's claims and nobody could touch it without his say-so. They were all in a right state. Some were saying it could make Sutter's look like child's play."

He paused and coughed, then spit a clot of blood on the ground right in front of him, at the feet of the women staring up at him. " 'Scuse me, ladies." He smiled and nodded at them. On his face the smile from his split top lip was more of the leer of a lecherous drunk twice his age. He breathed deeply once, twice, closed his eyes, and resumed his tale.

"Well when I got to this town and I seen that very same big fella playing at being a blacksmith, and him with his nice wifey and house and kid and all, why I knew he didn't need those claims no more'n I needed a busted nose." He turned his head to me and actually winked.

It was then I noticed that Finchy had slipped through the crowd and now stood at the front, his shotgun held in front of him.

"So I watched the big bastard," continued the marshal, "for signs that he'd head back out there. But he never did. I got tired of waiting for him to get off the pot, figured the claims would get played out again, so I tried to reason with him. He denied it, all right. Fought pretty hard, too. Never meant to do him harm, but he wouldn't listen to reason. Never did find them claim deeds that night."

"Burl never was out to Nevada," said Finchy, shaking a tense fist. "He barely ever left this town in all his twenty-some-odd years. I knowed him, his ma and pa, both dead, God rest 'em. Slim and Burl was the best of friends. You kilt the wrong man . . . marshal!" He spat the last word as if it pinched his tongue.

Clem's voice cracked the silence. "So we hired a killer to find himself?"

The marshal laughed and nodded. "Looks like it, Clem. And you were such a desperate sight, I tell you. 'Please Mr. Lawman, save our town. We need your help. Please help us!' Bunch of squallin' babies is all you are. But I did what you asked me to do. Then I took up with that pretty little thing old Burl left behind. Yessir, hard case, she was. Didn't fancy me, I reckon."

"But Burl wasn't the man you thought he was," said a little bald man behind Clem.

"No, that's true enough. But then again, looks like there's plenty of that goin' around."

I looked at Finchy, his bottom jaw quavering in hatred.

"Then you killed the boy and his ma," I said, prompting him.

"I reckon so," he stretched his good arm above his head, and sighed as if he'd awakened. "That boy was too clever for his own self. And as for his mama, well she needed a man all right. That's all I can say about that." He winked at the crowd. If ever there was a man with a wish for death at the hands of a mob, it was this character. He looked out over them and smiled as if he remembered something. "Say, I wonder where that big ol' fella with the claims is now?"

"You'll never find out," I said, waving the pistol from him toward the steps.

"I reckon not," he said, and lunged at me, swinging his wounded arm into play. He barreled into me and drove me backward. We piled through the multi-pane glass window of the general store and landed in a mass of razor-sharp shards, rolling and punching at each other on the slicing, glittering floor. In the crash I lost my grip on the revolver, but I managed to land a punch to his wounded shoulder. That winced him enough for me to knee him off me.

As we struggled, images of that old blind, silverback grizzly popped into my mind. It was a fight just like this, I thought. But I had won that fight, barely. I struggled hard with the marshal, and felt my strength leaving me. It was no good. Without sleep or food or water a man is a man in spirit only. And even the spirit flags without a little help now and then. I saw a blur of bloodied face, saw my own arms, slashed and bleeding and striking wildly, saw a grizzly with glowing eyes and a mouthful of fangs descending on me and then I heard a tremendous throaty growl. From which one of us, I'll never know.

Somehow I managed to push the marshal aside and it was enough room for Finchy to pull both triggers. The shotgun emptied itself into the murderer's chest. As the sound and smoke fought for escape from the store's front room, I dragged myself backward from under the dead man's legs and used the end of the counter to regain my feet. I looked down on the marshal. He'd lost that smile — and a whole lot more. His mouth was open wide as if in mid-growl, his white eyes bore a look of shock.

"I give him both barrels," said Finchy when the sound and smoke had drifted on. "One for the mother, one for her boy." He looked at the marshal as if at a mangled snake. "Should have had three barrels."

Nobody said anything else. I crunched through bits of shattered glass and Finchy helped me step over the window sill and out onto the porch.

"Well all right," I said, looking back in at the end of it all.

Finchy slapped my shoulder. "You got the last word . . . all right." He winked at me.

CHAPTER SIXTEEN

"How's Slim?" I asked him.

"He's gonna make it, I swear. He's twice as tough as nails."

And plenty big, too, I thought. "Finchy, there's something I have to do."

"What's that?"

"Take care of that poor man in the street up there." We both looked to the rumpled body on the ground at the far end of the main avenue. "I made a promise."

He nodded and said, "I understand that." Then he turned to me and said, "Can it wait 'til you've had a meal? I'd be right proud to have you at our table. Besides, you're all done in."

"I thank you, Finchy. But if I stop now I won't wake up for two days."

"Okay then. Count me in."

"And me," said a voice behind us. It was Slim. And he was smiling.

"Now boy, you been all stoved in. I don't

reckon your Ma's gonna think too highly of me if'n I —"

"Pa," said the big man, "I ain't a kid anymore. 'Sides, it's like the man says. If I stop now, I'll be out for better part of a week. Best to keep movin', get the job done."

Finchy scratched his temple, winked at me, and said to Slim, "Grab yourself a shovel then, boy. I'll roust some horses."

I stood there a moment more looking down at the dead marshal, the townsfolk keeping clear of me, some drifting back to their homes, none saying a word. A stray gust of cold morning air played through a thatch of his pale, sandy hair that the women had liked so well.

For years after, some little gesture, a detail — a confident tone, a hand movement, a bit of broken glass — would get me to thinking about that murderous brute. I would wonder how any one man could be heartless enough to yawn about the misery he brought to so many people's lives. There most definitely was something wrong with him. But then I would think of that savage crowd and I'd think that maybe he wasn't all that different from the rest of us.

But it can work the other way, too. I know because for a minute there when he came

to the cell in the middle of that night with a
fresh murder on his mind and the scratches
of a desperate woman on his face, I saw his
chest beating harder, heard that frantic edge
to his voice, saw the flawed, scared, cracked
human behind the façade of bravado. And
that brief memory gives me more hope on a
cold, lonely night for the future of human-
ity than all the shame-faced apologies I
received following the incident for the three
days that I stayed around Tall Pine.

CHAPTER SEVENTEEN

In the end we used the mute's own horse to carry him. We found it wandering not too far from the bay I rode, past the last building of Main Street. Someone had covered the battered man's body with a blanket and I used this to wrap his limp form. We bundled him on his horse and rode back up the street toward the crowd. I sat the bay and Finchy and Slim were astride their own horses. As it should be, Slim's was a giant of a beast with hooves like stove lids and more suited to field work than riding great distances. The crowd parted as we walked up and Clem stepped forward and grasped the bay's bridle. We stopped.

"We'll take care of him," he said, motioning to the dead man trailing behind me. "Give him a proper Christian burial in our town plot and all."

"No," I said and nodded toward the broken storefront where inside the marshal still lay sprawled in a smear of glass and blood. "You do that for him. As Christian as you can stand. Otherwise you'll never be any different than him."

Clem's hand dropped to his side and he nodded slowly, still looking at me. I hoped he understood. There wasn't much more I could say.

I'd be lying if I said I wanted to go back up there in the hills overlooking the town and bury the two brothers. It wouldn't have taken too much persuading to get me to put it off for a day, but something inside told me that was not the right way to go about it. I've often been pleasantly surprised in life by the good results of doing the right thing. It's gotten so that I figure, come what may, I'll follow my instincts first and worry about the results later. But I sure looked forward to some of Finchy's wife's cooking. The smells of that chicken and coffee had stayed with me since that night at the jail cell when I was denied their heavenly promise.

It took us a couple of hours to get back up there. I felt bad about putting the bay back into action, but in his own way he was as game as Tiny Boy. My thoughts turned from my stolen horse to my stolen gear.

Since the marshal had lured the brothers up into the woods with the expectation that they would return to town, the bulk of their gear, and so my gear, should be back in Tall Pine somewhere. Plenty of time to track it down.

My companions barely talked, much to my surprise. I expected Finchy to chatter the entire trip. Not until we left the little valley's rolling prairie and the terrain grew steeper and the trees grew thicker and taller did he speak. "Mother and I used to ride up here, back in the old days before anybody else come through, and take in all this beauty. Ain't been up this way much since you were a little one, Slim. Been too busy, I reckon."

I didn't mean to, but I laughed a little, despite the task at hand.

"What so funny?" said Finchy, not smiling.

"I'm sorry. But you called Slim 'little' and I'm having a hard time working that one over in my mind."

For a moment they were both quiet, and I thought I had stepped over some unseen line. I was about to blame it on my lack of sleep when a big, deep-chested laugh erupted from Slim and echoed right down the valley below us. Finchy gave into that infectious sound and I followed suit. It felt good to laugh. Almost as good as a hot meal and some sleep. Almost.

CHAPTER EIGHTEEN

We made it to the clearing with little error in direction. Before we got there I explained what I knew of the brothers to my companions and of what we would find there. I feared that animals might have savaged the boy's body, but all was as it should be. Not that the scene was easy to take. Death, and especially the results of violent death, are bitter things.

I slid the boy's gunbelt off and pried the pistol from his hand. No one need be buried with such a thing. I looked in their pockets for anything that might tell us who they were, where they came from, or if they had any family. But I found nothing of the sort. The boy's filthy bowler hat lay a few feet away and I tucked it onto his head. It occurred to me then, staring down at his dead body, that I didn't know his name. His brother certainly never told me.

We dug a grave deep enough and laid

194

them together. Finchy insisted that they each have a hand resting on the other. "They was brothers. Family's always got to stay in touch."

I thought briefly of the family I never had, of the hole in the ground that one day would bear me and no one else. A hardness grew in my throat and I forced it down. I arranged the blanket over them and Finchy stepped to the head of the grave before I had a chance to speak. He bowed his head and said, "It's a cruel world, Lord knows. Crueler to some than others. May these two fellers find a kinder place than the one they left. I expect they've earned it." Finchy looked at me and nodded.

I said, "Amen."

Slim whispered, "Good luck, boys. Amen," and turned away for a few minutes.

We all helped cover them with dirt, and then we gathered rocks and arranged a cairn over them to keep out the varmints. When we finished, we looked at the grave and Finchy said, "We'll make a proper marker, if you'd like."

"Thanks, yes. I think that would be the right thing to do," I said.

"What'll we put on it?" said Slim.

I thought for a moment, then said, "If we don't find both their names in their things back in town, how about, 'Here lie two brothers. Speak no evil.' "

CHAPTER NINETEEN

"So how did you know the marshal was back at the stable?" I asked Finchy as we plodded along back to his place. None of us, the horses included, had much urge to work up a sweat getting there.

"Nothing added up after you showed in town. Then I got hit on the noggin, and when I come around I wondered how there come to be jail cell keys on the floor next to me. But mostly I wanted a word with him 'bout mistreating my baby boy last night. That's when I seen him slink off from the crowd."

He raised his voice and looked over at his son, who was having a hard time keeping his chin from touching his chest. His head jerked upright, his eyes snapped open.

"Imagine clubbin' him and taking that shotgun." Finchy winked at me. "I give it to Slim for his nights working at the saloon."

I slowed my pace. My act wasn't fooling

anybody, least of all Finchy, but I tried to change the subject just the same. "So that's how you came to have shells for the gun. What would you have done if the shotgun hadn't been there?"

"Oh," he said, rubbing his own sore head. "I reckon I would have muckled onto that marshal barefisted."

I didn't say anything, but thanked my stars for the shotgun.

"You look doubtful," said Finchy, peering at me. "I can still get my licks in," he puffed upright in the saddle all of his five-and-a-half feet.

"After what we've been through, Finchy," I said. "I have no doubts about you whatsoever."

He nodded. We rode in silence for a few more minutes, then I asked, "Why weren't you ever marshal, Finchy? You seem to be the logical choice." I looked over at Slim and said, "And you've got one formidable deputy ready-made." The big man smiled in his half-doze. Even in a half-doze he was as alert as his father.

"Thought crossed my mind. Truth is, they never asked. Comes a time in a man's life when he shouldn't have to ask. He should be asked instead. Comes a time he waits to hear his friends ask him if they can do something for him instead of always the other way 'round."

It seems I probed a raw nerve. I nodded and we rode the rest of the trip to his house in silence. His notion of a favor from his friends said an awful lot about the type of man he was. Most people would regard being a marshal as a favor to the town and not the opposite. He was one of a kind and I got the sense that his son was much the same.

We finally made it to his spread, a tidy ranch house with a long porch, three rockers, and a chimney pushing out a steady thread of smoke. I took that as a good sign. The place was well kept with chickens in the yard and a small barn the right distance from the house. They had put a lot of thought and effort into the place and it showed.

"Here's home," said Finchy, dismounting halfway between the house and barn. I did the same and Slim took our reins. "I'll take care of the horses. Be right in."

I made to go with him, but Finchy pulled my arm and said, "He's a big boy. He can handle it."

We clumped across the porch and he pushed open the front door. "Mother, we're home."

Inside, an enormous woman smiled at us from a cookstove laden with bubbling pots and the most luscious food smells I have ever, or will ever, come across. I was a little hesitant to enter, unsure of the reality of the scene before me.

"Everything gonna be okay, Papa?" the massive woman said to Finchy.

"Oh, little doll, everything's working out fine." He kissed her on the cheek and she pushed him away as if they were courting kids who got caught in the orchard.

I was still a tad concerned about Slim. Did he know I was the one who clipped him on the head in the store room? Had he just been polite so far, waiting for a chance to get me alone?

I didn't have long to wait. He came in from dealing with the horses and his mother fluttered about him, making little cooing noises and escorting him to a big pine trestle table and a small wooden chair that squeaked in stress as he lowered himself into it. Before he could protest she had shucked the old ratty dressing from his head and he was sporting a head freshly bandaged the same as his father's, with a shocking amount of muslin wrapped and tapering to a point at the top.

When she finished he got up, the chair

squawked again, this time in relief, and crossed into the kitchen. "I want to tell you how sorry I am 'bout your head an' all," he said as he stuck out a massive hand. We shook, my own hand invisible, gripped in his.

I was confused. Too tired. I'm not hearing right, I thought. Then I remembered when we met in the bar and the clunk on the head he gave me on the day all of this began. I nodded. "And yours," I managed. "Took a nasty knock, I see."

"Yep," said Finchy, slapping the big brute on the back, "but mother set him right. She'll tend your head and that grazin' you took to the chest, too, of course. Can't sit down to the table without that being taken care of."

Why can't I? I wanted to shout. The intense aromas of warm foods in the warm kitchen were rapidly overwhelming me, but they were all staring at me, three smiles on three of the kindest faces I had come across in years of wandering the West.

Slim said, "Only thing I can't figure is why the marshal would break into the bar and steal the shotgun and club me with it? Not like he didn't have plenty of weapons of his own in the jail house."

"Now son, don't go to thinking about it

201

too hard yet. You took a right wallopin' on the bean. Set down at the table and get your strength back and by and by it'll come to you."

Finchy winked at me and pointed to a chair. "Set yourself down. It appears we're all a little addled right now. Some of Mother's fixins might go a long way to making things right."

"First things first, Papa." The enormous woman, still smiling, patted the same chair and picked up her scissors and the roll of muslin. I looked to the stove, where a coffee pot steamed and thick stew bubbled, and to the countertops where loaves of bread and mounds of biscuits and pies — I lost count after the fourth — all waited to be eaten. What was in the oven I couldn't be sure, but I think it may have been a chicken or two. Maybe a roast. With potatoes and thick gravy.

I turned back to the family, all three of them still smiling at me. I sat down and she dabbed my wounds clean and wrapped my head in muslin. The things I do for a hot meal.

CHAPTER TWENTY

Two days later I was standing at the livery at the western end of Main Street loading my found gear onto my found horse. It didn't take much persuading to make the man who'd bought him from the brothers realize Tiny Boy belonged with me and would be leaving with me, free of charge. I did tip him for taking care of Tiny Boy.

I took from the dead brothers' piled possessions what was mine. The only missing items that I replicated from their own stocks were a few pieces of tinware and what cash I found, which still didn't amount to the money they'd pilfered from me. But that was water under the bridge.

We found no addresses or names of any kind, and so I did not feel badly about taking from their traps what I guessed I would need. I wanted to change out of the too-large shirt that Finchy's wife had insisted I take. It was one she had made for Slim from his younger years, and though I am a large man myself, it billowed on me. I couldn't bring myself to shuck it just yet.

Finchy accompanied me about my tasks, helping where he could, and quite disappointed that I would not take cash from the sale of the remainder of their gear. I insisted that he keep it. He said he would put it into a special kitty for some families he knew who might need a little help beyond what his farm could offer. He winked and touched his nose.

I did help myself to the brothers' food stocks and ammunition. I figured they owed me that much. I also found my revolvers, my rifle, my little coin purse (empty), and even my knife and belt from the marshal's office. The rest of my gear was pretty much intact, save for my books. They weren't among the gear. I inquired at the mercantile, where used goods were regularly traded, but I was greeted with confused headshakes. I asked where the brothers had slept and was pointed toward the bordello. I looked through the room they rented, but there was no sign of my beloved tomes. The prostitute I awakened in the room was perplexed and asked me twice, yawning, if I was sure it wasn't something other than books I was looking for.

I guessed she was half my age and had less than half of her teeth left. Her ratty blond hair hung limp and shineless and she had scabbed knuckles. Her wrist bones were painful to look at. Her eyes were dark, sunken eggs with no fervor for life in them. Fewer sights are sadder than an old-before-her-time prostitute in the bright glare of early morning.

It may be that that's the only sort of woman I am able to attract given that I am less than pretty myself to most people I meet, but I prefer to stay true to my ongoing quest to lose myself forever in the West. Such invitations, or those for companionship or friendship from any people I meet, are far between on my journey. I partake of few, and none of those for very long, but they are markers, milestones along the way. Toward where, I have no idea.

She flopped backward on the bed and curled up on her side, already half asleep. She looked like a tiny, malnourished bird. I touched my hat brim and nodded to her. I whispered, "Good luck," and closed the door behind me as I left.

By the time I got back down to the street, empty handed, I had raised a few eyebrows. Let them think what they will, I thought. Telling them I was looking for books in a bordello would be akin in their eyes to a wolf telling a rooster that he was looking for a mouthful of hay in the chicken coop.

As the following days had slumped back into familiar routine for the townsfolk, so their embarrassment and humility of two days before visibly abated. They looked eager to forget the incident. And I sensed a tone of urgency in the air as evidenced by the pained, nervous looks on their faces as they all stared at me.

The irony of the situation wasn't lost on me. Plain fact was that most people liked the marshal. He was a charismatic person who gave everyone in the small, struggling town a sense of optimism. He was handsome, he spoke well, kept a clean and tidy appearance, and he always made a good impression. I, on the other hand, walked into town the day a child was murdered looking every inch as though I had been mauled by a bear. Even on the best of days my looks don't help my case any.

I swung up onto Tiny Boy and sat there, back in my own saddle on my own horse for the first time in a long, long week. And it felt right. Finchy looked up at me with envy or pity in his eyes. Or a little of both. There was also something I hadn't seen in quite a while and that was kindness writ large and easy on the man's craggy features.

Clem, as I expected, was appointed town spokesman. He stood back a couple of yards with his arms folded across his chest. "We been talking and we decided that we could use a new marshal. You're a big fella. And we know you can handle a gun." He looked around him and a few folks forced dry laughs here and there. "Maybe you'd like to take on the job?"

I was about to say something about being flattered, but instead I sat there for a few moments. Clem shifted on his feet, unfolded his arms, and put his hands in his pants pockets.

"You're forgetting that a man has to like what he does," I said.

"You like whatever it is that you do?" He answered me too quickly.

Good point, I thought. I didn't have a good answer or a bad one. But I could tell by the looks of fear on their faces that they were offering me the job so they could tell themselves that come what may they had at least made the gesture. Guilt, and the thought of guilt that will have to be born for years to come, is a terrible thing. I know. I carry my own share of it. And I will forever, just like those townsfolk.

I shook my head. "No. Thanks just the

same. It isn't for me. And I'm not so sure everyone here shares your way of thinking. Besides, you already have a marshal and you don't even know it."

Finchy looked away, out of town toward the rolling hills and shook his head. I knew he hadn't wanted me to say anything, but sometimes people need a nudge.

Clem looked behind him at the faces of his fellow townsfolk. They weren't sure what emotion to show. But I could read those faces. They all knew exactly who I meant. I had a lot of practice in reading faces, in figuring out what people were thinking. I can usually tell more from the first flicker of emotion that passes over a face than from the mask that is pulled on just after it. They'd probably get around to offering the job to Finchy. And I was pretty sure he'd take them up on it — after a sufficient cool period.

"Well, what is it you would like from us?" I swear he almost sighed.

Truth be told, up to that point I didn't want a damn thing from any of them. I was anxious to depart as soon as possible from this strange little lost town. I knew that the sideways looks I received ever since riding in that morning with Finchy were looks of desperation that urged me to leave. Those looks told me that until I left their town for good, they could not begin to forget what they had done. Part of me didn't want them to ever forget.

Somewhere in the dankest unswept corner of their minds there would remain alive all their days the knowledge that they had behaved in the worst way a human can. I'd like to say that was enough for me. Though I wanted to ride out of there with nary a parting look, now that Clem had tossed in arrogance a scrap at my feet with which to buy down their guilt, I found the opportunity too ripe. I even allowed myself to embrace the idea of staying in the dark little place. I knew I would never do so, but to consider the thought was satisfying.

What did I want? The possibilities lined up in my mind like scrubbed schoolchildren in their Sunday best, each one full of the promise of a life yet to be lived. I'm afraid I smiled then and said, "It didn't escape me that you're out a blacksmith." I raised my eyebrows in innocent inquiry and looked at the faces of the small crowd. "I have some experience in that area. You said yourself that I'm a big fellow."

The slight desperation that had worked their faces moments before now turned to outright fear. They knew they couldn't stop me from staying, felt they owed me some sort of debt for helping rid their town of an unsavory character, but they didn't want me there, wouldn't ever get past my ravaged features. And I knew it. I was toying with them, and as cruel as it sounds, a part of me enjoyed it.

People try, but they don't change. Hell, they can't change. I should know, I tried for years. When I gave up and accepted that who I am is who I am, warts and all, I slept better. Folks can alter their ways for a time but they'll always slip back to who they were. And some of these people would eventually welcome back into their lives another handsome savior, though maybe not in the form of a marshal. But if someone handsome and clever and with all the right answers came along, some of these folks would fall right in step behind him the same as they would always look at me and see someone who bothers them in their heads somehow. It's the way of the world.

I stared down at them from atop Tiny Boy and looked right into Clem's eyes. I thought for a minute, then I turned in my saddle and said to all of them, "I'd like to be treated as though I belonged here." The people stared, their smiles long gone. I fooled myself into thinking that there was a sliver of a moment before the smiles faded when I could have sworn they'd accepted me for who I am. A little bit of me liked the idea just fine — to be welcomed into their little nest.

But no, that moment passed and slipped somewhere into my mind quietly to wait for some cold night when I'm crouched over a fire that I can't coax any bigger and my hands are numb and I'm so lonely I'd trade my own two legs for a conversation and a cup of coffee. Then I'd pull that little sliver out from where it's been stuck in my brain and go over the possibilities again, as painful as it always would be.

"I want people to look at me and smile," I said. "I want to be asked in for a piece of pie somewhere, because I'm a man who looks like he's been rode hard and put up wet. I'd like it for kids to not run off when they see me coming or for women on the sidewalks to not put their hands to their throats and look for the nearest shop and then duck inside until I pass. I'd like for shopkeeps to not flip their 'Open' signs over in the middle of the day because it looks like I might be headed their way. I'd like range bosses to hire me because I come with good, hard-won references, and judging from my traps they can tell I've been around

211

a cow a time or two. I'd like to be given the chance to prove myself before being judged."

Clem looked as if he were trying very hard to understand someone speaking in a foreign tongue. His eyes scrunched, he let out a long breath through his nose, definitely a sigh that time, and finally he said, "I'm thinking a sum of money could be arranged. Something like that should appeal to a traveling man such as yourself, who obviously doesn't appear to want to give up his freedom and settle down. Certainly you'd find our little town boring, to say the least. No, no, I'm thinking of good, old, cold, hard cash. How would that suit you?" He smiled, a pink hand reached into his vest pocket and came out pinching the top of a little tied sack of coins. He cupped it in both hands as if presenting a baby chick to me.

I closed my eyes, inhaled deeply, let out my breath slowly, and said, "How 'bout a plate of potatoes covered in thick beef gravy. And a cup of good, strong coffee." I opened my eyes. The townspeople stared at me. So I nodded to Finchy and Slim, reined that big horse west, and headed on out of that town.

No sir, some things would never change.

CPSIA information can be obtained
at www.ICGtesting.com
Printed in the USA
FFOW05n1801300714